# EVE
## OF THE
## DEAD

# EVE OF THE DEAD

**A TALE OF
APOCALYPTIC TERROR BY
NATHAN TUCKER**

MOORHEN PRESS

# EVE OF THE DEAD

All Rights Reserved © 2007 by Nathan Tucker

This story is a work of fiction. All the characters and events portrayed in this story are either fictitious or used fictitiously. Any resemblance to actual persons, whether living or dead, is purely coincidental.

No part of this book may be reproduced or transmitted in any form or by any means without written permission of the publisher.

ISBN-13: 978-0-6151-6965-1
ISBN-10: 0-615-16965-1

Published by Moorhen Press

First Edition

*"I saw the dead, the great and the small, standing before the throne, and they opened books.
Another book was opened, which is the book of life. The dead were judged out of the things which were written in the books, according to their works."*

Revelation 20:12

# 1

The city skyline formed a jagged silhouette against the brilliant orange sky at sunset. Dark, purple-tinted clouds loomed in the horizon. The city streets were eerily quiet as discarded newspapers and other small trash fluttered along the empty sidewalks and alleyways in the cool, gentle breeze. Abandoned vehicles lined the roads, rusting away as if they had been sitting there for a thousand years.

The scenery looked strangely familiar to the man who stood silently observing. But something was missing. It was a scene from his recent past, the same location he had stood only a few short months ago. The view stood out in stark contrast to the way he had remembered it. All of the people were missing. The vast landscape was now desolate—devoid of any human activity. It was like a strange dream.

Distant sounds of drums and buzzing guitars gradually became louder and clearer as Mark Walker began to emerge from his sleep. For a moment, he had forgotten where he was, but he quickly remembered where he had dozed off. He was sitting on the old familiar couch in the shed—or the *jam room*, as he liked to call it.

His older brother, Scott, had recently converted the wooden shed in their parents' backyard into a practice-room for their band. Lately, their friends had been coming over almost every night to play.

"You want another brewski?" a voice shouted over the sound of the loud rock music. A sweaty hand holding a green bottle of Rolling Rock beer hovered in front of Mark's face. Mark wiped the sleep from his bloodshot eyes and looked up. Joe Simmons was standing over him with an inebriated grin on his face.

"Sure, man," Mark replied, and he grabbed the bottle and popped the top off with his teeth. "Thanks."

Joe staggered over to his bass guitar and put the strap over his shoulder. Beads of sweat clung to his freckled face in the small, humid building. He pushed his wavy blonde hair off his forehead, chiming in on the bass to the song that Scott and his cousin, Luke, were playing.

Mark slouched back on the couch, drinking his beer as he listened to the band's loud music. He wondered where Sean Turner, the rhythm guitarist had gone. Then the door to the shed opened, and the bright-orange evening sunlight filled his eyes.

The silhouette of a man carrying an electric guitar on his back appeared in the doorway.

"Hey," Sean said, pushing his shaggy auburn hair behind his ears as he stepped into the dimply-lit room. "Are you getting hungry yet?" Fair-skinned and thin, he stood almost as tall as Mark as he stepped up into the wooden building.

"I sure as hell am," Mark replied. "Let's get a pizza from Goodfella's." Goodfella's was the only pizza shop in the small town.

"Sounds like a plan," Sean said. He walked in front of Scott's drum set, waving a hand in the air.

Scott stopped playing the drums, followed by Joe's bass, and finally Luke's guitar. Feedback squealed noisily from Luke's amplifier for a moment. Then he turned down the volume, pushing his plastic-rimmed glasses up on his nose as he knelt down.

"What's up?" the shirtless drummer asked, scratching his tattooed arm with his drumsticks in hand.

"You guys wanna pitch in for a pizza?" Sean asked.

"Sure," the others mumbled. They reached into their pockets and pulled out several dollar bills before handing them to Sean.

"We'll be back in a few," Sean said as he took the money.

Mark guzzled his last sip of beer and followed the red-haired man out the door.

"You okay to drive?" Mark asked.

Sean nodded, and the two men walked to the gold 1985 Toyota van that was parked in the driveway.

The van was old, but it still ran well. It had power windows, power locks, a sunroof, and a mini-refrigerator between the front seats. The rear bumper had a little damage from a minor fender-bender several years back, but overall, it was in relatively good condition.

Sean cranked the engine and it started up right away. He rolled down the tinted windows, revved the engine, and put it in reverse. From the corner of his eye, he caught a glimpse of Mark lighting up a cigarette.

"Hey man," Sean said. "Put that shit out."

"What?" Mark asked.

"No smoking in the *Babe Mobile*."

"Damn, I forgot."

"You really ought to quit smoking those things," Sean suggested as he steered out onto the main road. The darkness had begun to creep in, so he turned on his headlights.

"I know," Mark replied as he flicked the butt out the window. "It's a dirty habit." He thought about his nights playing rock shows in the smoky Atlanta nightclubs where he had picked up the habit.

*Things were different there*, he thought to himself as he gazed out at the trees along rural country road. *It's so much more peaceful here.*

At twenty-one, Mark was a very big man. He stood six-foot, three-inches tall and weighed two-hundred and forty-three pounds. He had let his curly brown hair grow out while he was away.

He had lived in the small, rural town of Crawfordville, Florida for most of his life. But at the age of twenty he had moved to Atlanta, Georgia for a brief period of time. While living in the big city, he sang in a hard rock cover-band, playing a number of shows to pay his bills. However, the band didn't stay together very long.

After his band broke up, he had trouble finding a decent-paying job, so he reluctantly took a job working the graveyard-shift at a local fast-food restaurant. This job did not last long either. After working for only a few weeks, he was robbed at gunpoint. That was the last straw for Mark. He quit the job and moved back home to Florida.

Soon after returning home, his older brother, Scott, and his childhood friends asked him to join their band, *The Exploding Heads*, as the lead singer.

Now, only two months after returning home to his friends and family, Mark was content. He gazed out of the window at the lush scenery, daydreaming about his surreal experiences in the big city—so far away and different from little town of Crawfordville.

Suddenly, something smashed loudly into the windshield, pulling Mark back to reality.

Sean slammed on the brakes, causing the wheels to lock up. Smoke rose from the rubber tires as the van skidded to a screeching stop.

The two men looked at each other, startled.

"What the hell was that?" Mark yelled.

There was a huge crack in the windshield and red liquid was splattered on the glass. The two men stared at the bloody windshield in horror for a moment. Then Sean pulled over to the side of the road and put the van into park. Slowly, the two men opened their doors and got out of the van.

"Jesus!" Sean shouted, stopping dead in his tracks. "We hit somebody!" The limp, twisted body of a man in a white t-shirt lay in the middle of the dimly lit road only a few yards away.

"Is he...*dead*?" Mark asked, his voice cracking.

"I don't know!" Sean cried.

The two young men walked cautiously toward the body in the street. Sean cringed as he noticed the man's legs were bent backward toward his head in an awkward contortion. It looked as though his spine had snapped in half at his lower-back. Blood was running from his nose and the sides of his mouth.

The two men crouched down beside the injured man.

"I can't tell if he's breathing," Sean said, his heart beating anxiously. "Can you?"

Before Mark could reply, the bright headlights of a car suddenly shined on them as it pulled up behind the van and parked. Mark stood up, holding his hand over his brow to shield his eyes from the bright lights. He spotted two large unlit lights on top of the car—a red one and a blue one.

"Shit, man," he whispered. "It's a cop!"

The car sat silently for a minute, bathing the young men in the bright light of its headlamps. The two men stood rigid as they eyed the vehicle nervously. Then the driver door of the deputy sheriff's car creaked open, and a uniformed officer stepped out.

"What seems to be the problem, gentleman?" the officer enquired, shining his flashlight at the men's faces.

Sean's hands began to tremble and he hesitated for a moment before speaking. He swallowed anxiously, shielding his eyes from the light with the palm of his hand.

"Well, um..." he stumbled over his words. "This man came out of nowhere..."

The deputy shined his flashlight at the motionless body of the man on the ground.

"I think we... I think we *hit* him," Sean gasped.

The officer leaned his head over to his CB radio and mumbled something into the microphone piece. He looked back up at the two men and held out his hand.

"Just stay calm, all right?" the deputy cautioned. "Help is on the way."

Suddenly, the man on the ground let out a loud groan. Startled, Sean and Mark backed away as the officer hurried over to the man's side. Kneeling down, he checked the man's pulse.

"Can you hear me, sir?" the officer asked. The man groaned again, lifting one of his arms. "Just stay calm, sir! You were in a bad accident."

Suddenly, the man grabbed the back of the police officer's head and smashed his face into the pavement. Then he bit the deputy on his neck, shaking his head around violently as he ripped out a chunk of flesh with his bare teeth. A stream of blood squirted out from the officer's neck as he screamed in agony.

"Shit!" Mark yelled.

The deputy stood up quickly and shoved the man off of him, but the man grabbed his leg and bit into his calf muscle. The officer pulled out his handgun and fired a quick shot into the top of the man's head, tearing a hole in his skull. The man's body dropped limply on the pavement as the officer dropped his gun and fell backwards onto the road. He clenched the gaping wound in his neck with one hand, and reached out toward Sean and Mark with the other.

"Call for help!" the deputy cried. He unhooked the radio from his shirt with one hand as he held his wounded neck with the other. "Hurry, I'm bleedin' bad!"

Mark grabbed the radio that was attached to the officer's belt via a wire. He leaned over the deputy and held the radio up to his mouth.

"Somebody help!" Mark yelled frantically into the microphone. "Somebody help! Officer down! We need help!" He waited and listened to the receiver. Waves of static blasted from the speaker for a moment. Then the voice of a woman came over the radio.

"Where are you located, sir?" the voice asked.

Sean bent down and put his hand on the officer's head. "He's dead!" he exclaimed.

The two men froze up, staring at the lifeless police officer, unable to speak.

"Sir?" the voice came over the radio. "Are you there?"

Suddenly, the policeman's eyes opened, staring wildly at the night sky.

"Oh, shit!" Mark yelled.

The officer grabbed Mark's leg and tried to bite it, but Mark shook him off and backed away. The deputy crept slowly toward the two men, reaching out with one arm and groaning.

"Are you there, sir?" the voice said again over the police radio. The officer reached out and grabbed Sean's foot as he opened his mouth.

"Get his gun!" Sean screamed as he kicked the officer in the face, causing him to lose his grip on Sean's foot. Mark ran over to the policeman's Glock pistol and picked it up off the ground.

"Dude," Mark said, pointing the gun at the deputy as he backed away. "Let's get the hell out of here!" The two men retreated slowly for a moment, staring nervously at the horrible site on the ground. Then they took off running toward the van. Sean jumped in the driver's seat and started the engine. Mark jumped in the passenger side and slammed the door shut. The van peeled out onto the road in a cloud of dust.

"Let's get back to my house!" Mark cried as Sean gunned the engine.

"What the hell is going on?" Sean exclaimed, watching the speedometer climb above seventy.

"I don't know, man," Mark replied, shaking his head. "This is crazy!" He fumbled nervously through his shirt pocket and pulled out a cigarette. With trembling hands, he lit it, sucking the thick smoke deep into his lungs.

Sean took a deep breath and glanced in the rear-view mirror as he eased off the gas slightly. "Okay…" he paused. "We've got to stay calm."

"I could have sworn that cop was dead," Mark mumbled. The cigarette dangled from his mouth as he blew smoke through his nose. "He tried to bite me!" He was fidgeting with the pistol, pulling the magazine out and popping it back into the gun.

"Calm down!" Sean demanded. "Don't freak out on me! We've got to…"

"Look!" Mark interrupted suddenly, pointing through the windshield.

About a hundred yards ahead of the van, a car had smashed head-on into a telephone pole on the side of the road. Clouds of smoke rose from the hood of the car.

Sean turned on his overhead lights and slowed down as they approached the wreck. A shower of sparks erupted from a transformer on the telephone pole. As they got closer, they could see that the driver's door was wide open, and two men were crouched over a woman that was lying on the ground. The men's backs were turned the van, so Sean and Mark couldn't see their faces. Sean shined his headlights on the people as Mark rolled down his window and leaned his head out.

"Is she okay?" he asked the men, his voice trembling with adrenaline.

The two men lifted their heads slowly and turned around, shielding their eyes from the bright headlights. Blood dripped from their mouths, and they growled angrily at the van. One of the men was holding what appeared to be a half-eaten severed arm. As the men stood up, Mark noticed that the female driver's stomach was split wide-open, and blood and guts were spilling out onto the ground. There were bite marks all over her body.

"Shit!" Mark yelled.

Sean floored the gas pedal, speeding off onto the road again. After driving for another two or three miles, they reached Mark's house. Sean steered the van quickly into the driveway, slammed on the brakes, and threw it into park. The two men jumped out of the van and ran over to the shed where their friends were practicing. As they approached the little building, the muffled rock music grew louder and louder.

"Hey, you guys!" Mark tried to yell over the booming drums and buzzing guitars. He walked into the shed as Sean followed him, trying to catch his breath.

The band kept playing for a minute until Scott spotted Mark waving his arms around frantically. He stopped hitting the drums, but his cymbals rang out. Joe stopped playing the bass, followed by Luke, whose amp squealed loudly with feedback.

"Where's the pizza?" Scott asked, looking slightly annoyed.

"We hit somebody!" Mark cried.

"What?" Scott asked with a puzzled look.

Mark opened his mouth, but the words wouldn't come out. He paused and took a deep breath. "We were on our way to Goodfella's, and some dude just came out of nowhere… and we hit him!"

"You're shittin' me."

"No, I'm not!" Mark glanced over at Sean. "And that's not all!"

"A cop drove up," Sean said nervously.

"You hit the guy and took off?" Scott asked.

"No…" Sean replied, looking at the floor. His eyes darted over to Mark. "Well… sort of."

"The guy that we hit attacked the cop," Mark said. "And then the cop shot the dude!"

"What the hell?" Luke shouted.

Joe leaned his bass guitar against his amp. Feedback hummed from the speaker.

"Please tell me you're joking," Scott said, crossing his tattooed arms. He watched as Sean paced nervously in front of the shed.

"I'm serious!" Mark yelled. "Not only did the cop shoot the guy, but he also tried to attack us!"

"The cop attacked *you*?" Joe cut in.

"Yeah," Mark replied. "So we took off. And on the way back, we saw two guys…" He choked for moment as a wave of nausea overcame him. "…two guys…and they were eating somebody."

"*Eating* somebody?" Scott burst out with laughter. "Okay now I know you're just fucking with us."

"Look at me, Scott!" Mark yelled with wide eyes. "I'm serious!"

Scott stepped out of the shed and walked past Sean, who was still pacing back and forth. Luke and Joe stood silently beside their instruments and gave each other a puzzled look.

"We're not kidding around," Sean said as Scott walked by him. "They were like cannibals or something. They were really eating a dead woman."

"Oh, stop it," Scott replied sarcastically as he kept walking. "You're making me hungry."

In the distance, Scott spotted the dark figure of a man walking slowly toward the shed. The man appeared to be stumbling a little bit.

"Can I help you?" Scott asked the man. The man didn't reply, but kept staggering silently toward him.

"Hey!" Scott yelled. "Can you hear me? Are you drunk or something?"

Sean squinted, trying to get a clear image of the lurching figure in the darkness of the night. "He's one of those people!" he cried.

Scott ignored Sean's warning and walked closer to the man. As he approached, he could see the man's scraggly white hair and pale, wrinkled skin in the dim moonlight.

"This is private property, old man!" Scott warned. The man still didn't respond, but kept lurching forward, staring blankly at Scott. As he drew closer, he reached out with his long, skinny arms and tried to grab Scott.

"Shit, man!" Scott yelled. He punched the man square in the jaw. The powerful blow knocked the old man off his feet and he fell on his side.

"Scott!" Mark yelled from the shed as he ran toward his brother. "Get away from him!"

"Fuck you, old man!" Scott shouted, ignoring his brother. He kicked the man on the ground, but he barely flinched. Suddenly, the man grabbed Scott's foot with his boney hands and tried to bite his ankle.

"What the hell?" Scott yelled as he shook his leg loose from the man's frail grip and took a couple of steps back. The old man stood up, and moaned gruffly.

"Run, Scott!" Mark yelled as he arrived next to his brother, and pulled the pistol out of his jeans.

"Don't come any closer," Mark warned as he pointed the gun at the old man. "I'll blow your goddamn head off!"

The man stretched his arms out toward the two brothers and started walking menacingly toward them.

"I told you!" Mark cried, taking a step back. "Something ain't right!" He took another step back and bumped into his brother.

"Give me that gun!" Scott insisted and grabbed the gun from Mark's hand. He held the Glock up sideways and fired a shot, hitting the man in the chest. The bullet ripped a hole through the man's white shirt as thick blood sprayed out into the cool night air. The man flinched and staggered backward for a moment. His eyes stared blankly at the two brothers, and he let out a ghastly moan. Then he started walking toward them again with renewed vigor. Scott fired another shot, hitting the man on the right side of his throat.

Blood squirted out from the bullet wound, but the old man seemed to ignore it and continued lurching forward.

"Run, Scott!" Mark yelled.

Scott raised the gun in disbelief. "What the hell, man?" He aimed carefully at the slow-moving man and fired a clean shot directly into the man's forehead. Tiny pieces of skull fragments and brain matter flew through the air from the back of his head. The old man's neck jerked back sharply and his body collapsed limply to the ground.

The two brothers stared at the motionless body for a moment in utter disbelief of what had just happened. Then Scott stepped toward the body, eyeing it curiously, as he aimed the gun at the corpse.

"Let's go!" Mark yelled, and he grabbed the gun from Scott's hands. "Don't get near it."

Mark tucked the handgun into his jeans and the two brothers headed back to the shed, where they found that the door had been had shut. As they approached, Sean opened the door for them. Inside, Joe was anxiously guzzling a beer and Luke was on his cell phone.

"I can't get a signal," Luke said in a panicked voice. "There's no service! Somebody call nine-one-one!"

Joe sat his beer on an amp and pulled his cell phone out of his pocket. "What the hell?" he exclaimed. "I don't have a signal either!"

"I told you guys!" Sean yelled. "I told you we weren't kidding!"

"All right," Scott said. "Calm down! Everybody needs to calm down."

"Calm down?" Luke retorted, throwing his guitar onto the couch. "You just shot that guy!"

"Didn't you see anything?" Scott snapped. "He attacked me!"

"He was trying to kill us," Mark insisted as he peered out of the window. "He's just like those people that Sean and I saw earlier!"

"What the hell is going on?" Joe cried.

"I'm calling nine-one-one!" Luke yelled. "Let's go inside the house!"

"All right then," Mark agreed. "Let's go."

Sean cracked the door to the shed and peered out cautiously for a moment before opening it. Then he stepped outside and started walking quickly toward the two brothers' house. The other guys followed close behind.

Once they got inside, Luke headed straight for the kitchen. He picked up the cordless phone that was lying on the table and pressed the talk button.

"There's no dial-tone," Luke said. "The battery must be dead. Is there another phone in the house?"

"Yeah," Scott replied. "There's one in my parents' room."

Luke walked quickly through the living room and disappeared into the back of the house. The other four stayed in the kitchen.

"You didn't have to shoot that guy," Joe said angrily, looking at Scott.

"Just shut up about it, will ya?" Scott retorted.

"Where the hell did you get that gun?" Joe asked.

Scott looked at Mark, and Mark rolled his eyes.

"I told you..." Mark replied. "That cop tried to attack us earlier. We took his gun!"

Suddenly, Luke darted back into the kitchen. "I can't get through! Come listen to this!"

Sean pushed his way through the group and followed Luke through the living room, and Joe followed behind Sean.

Once they reached the master bedroom, Luke dialed 911 and handed the phone to Sean.

Sean put his ear to the phone as it rang several times. Then a recording answered.

"We're sorry," the message said, "but due to the high volume of calls we are receiving, no operators are currently available. Please stay on the line for the next available operator."

Sean waited for a few minutes, and then hung up. He offered the phone to Joe.

Joe pressed redial and listened to the message. "Jesus Christ!" he exclaimed. "What the hell's going on?"

Scott and Mark walked into the bedroom.

"What's going on?" Scott asked.

"We're just getting a recording when we call nine-one-one," Luke replied. "They must be flooded with calls."

"Where is everybody?" Joe asked, looking over at Scott. "Where is the rest of your family?"

"They went to Tallahassee," Scott replied. He paused and looked at the clock. "But they were supposed to be home three hours ago! Let me hold the phone."

Joe handed the phone to Scott, and Scott called his mother's cell phone.

"It's going not even going to her voicemail," Scott said. "That's strange."

"Let me call my parents," Luke said, reaching for the phone. Scott handed him the phone and he dialed his parents' number. He let it ring eleven times before hanging up.

"No one's answering at my house either," Luke said with a worried look on his face.

Sean and Joe both tried to call their families, but no one answered at either number.

"Something really strange is going on," Luke said, biting his thumbnail. "I'm going to keep trying nine-one-one."

"Let's check the news," Mark suggested. "If something big is happening, it should be on the local news."

Luke dialed 911 again, and the other four guys went back into the living room. Mark turned on the television. The screen lit up, but all that showed up was static. He flipped through the channels, but every channel he put it on was the same—snow.

"Damn it!" Mark exclaimed. "The cable's out."

"It might be because of that wreck we saw earlier," Sean said. "Remember, that woman hit a telephone pole."

"Why don't we try the radio?" Joe suggested.

"Good idea," Mark replied. He walked over to the entertainment center beside the television and turned on the radio. Static blasted from the speakers, and Scott turned the volume down a little bit. He changed the station, and the radio picked up a program.

"... *urges you to stay indoors. Do not go out onto the streets and do not leave your homes. Again, the authorities are issuing an order to stay inside and keep your doors locked until further notice.*"

"What the hell?" Scott exclaimed.

"Hush," Sean said, pressing his index finger to his mouth. "Listen..."

Mark turned up the volume.

"*We'll continue to stay on the air giving you up-to-the-minute reports as more details unfold. Please stay tuned for further instructions.*"

"What is this shit?" Scott shouted, raising his hands.

"Be quiet and listen!" Mark replied.

"*If you're just joining us, we're bringing you live coverage of the chaos unfolding here in Tallahassee. There has been a string of mass murders and anarchy reported all throughout the city. City officials are urging residents to stay indoors and keep their doors locked until further notice. It is unclear what exactly is happening, but there have also been national reports of similar events taking place. You're listening to eighty-eight point nine FM, WFSU radio— bringing you live coverage of this breaking news. Stay tuned for further coverage of this and related stories.*"

"Oh my god," Joe gasped. "This is crazy!"

Sean ran to the back door and locked it, and Luke locked the front door. Mark followed suit and hurried into the kitchen to the door leading to the carport. He locked both the doorknob and the bolt lock, and went back into the living room.

"Let me see that pistol," Scott said as Mark entered the room.

Mark retrieved the gun from his jeans and handed it to his brother. Scott held one hand under the grip of the gun and pressed the magazine-release button with his other thumb. The clip fell into his hand, and he examined it closely.

"It's a seventeen-round clip," he explained. "You have thirteen bullets left in the gun. We're gonna need a lot more than this if the shit hits the fan."

Scott popped the clip back in the Glock and handed it to Mark. He sighed, shaking his head, and walked upstairs.

Joe and Sean had been sitting in front of the radio, listening attentively with their ears practically glued to the speakers.

"Listen to this!" Joe cried, and turned up the volume.

*"...and these strange reports have included multiple eyewitness accounts of random acts of cannibalism being performed on the victims. We have received reports of killers eating their victims in the streets of Tallahassee and surrounding areas. These details cannot be confirmed, but the reports keep pouring in. We'll try to keep you informed on this when further information is obtained. Now let's go to our correspondent, Carol Anne Parker, who is on West Tennessee Street with live coverage of these events."*

"This is insane," Sean said, looking astonished. "It's just like what we saw earlier. Those guys were really eating that woman!"

"And that cop we saw earlier," Mark added. "He tried to bite us. And that crazy old man almost bit Scott!"

"We're definitely keeping the doors locked!" Joe exclaimed, with a chill in his voice.

As the three friends listened to the radio, Scott came back down the stairs into the living room. He had changed clothes, and was now wearing a black t-shirt and khaki pants. In one hand, he carried a Remington pump-action shotgun, and a box of shotgun shells in the other. He sat down in a large recliner in the living room and started loading shells into the gun.

"Nice," Sean said gleefully. "I didn't know you had a shotgun."

"Nobody fucks with my house," Scott replied, curling his upper lip. He loaded the fourth shell and cocked the gun.

"I'll go check on Luke," Joe said, standing up. He walked into the bedroom where Luke was sitting. Luke was still on the phone.

"Any luck?" Joe asked.

"No," Luke replied, looking forlorn. "I'm still on hold."

Joe looked at his cell phone again and noticed that it still had no service. "Just forget about it, man. You're tying up the line. What if our families try to call us?"

"You're right," Luke sighed, and hung up the phone. The two cousins walked down the dark hallway to the living room.

When they entered the room, Mark was getting some blankets and pillows out of the closet, and Sean was still listening intently to the radio. Scott was sitting in the recliner, clenching his shotgun in his folded arms while he rocked gently in the chair.

"It's getting late," Mark said as he spread some blankets out on the floor. "Maybe we should get some sleep."

"I'll stay up and keep watch if you guys want to sleep," Scott offered.

"Sounds good to me," Mark replied, and he sat down on the couch. "I can barely keep my eyes open." He leaned his head back and rubbed his eyes, yawning. He pulled his handgun out of his jeans and set it on the end table, and then laid back.

"Same here," Joe agreed. "All that beer is catching up with me." He lay down on his back on one of the pallets. Luke laid on one of the other blankets.

Sean turned the volume down a little bit on the radio, and then leaned back against the couch. After a few minutes, his eyes began to grow heavy, and he lay down on a pallet.

The radio continued to broadcast the news quietly as the four men slowly dozed off to sleep. Scott sat listening to the radio, cradling his shotgun in his folded arms.

# 2

"Yes, that's right, Tom. I'm standing at the intersection of Ocala and West Tennessee Street, just yards away from the scene of a multiple homicide."

"Can you tell us what happened, and do you know what the motive was behind these crimes, Carol?"

"Well, Tom, we do know that the there were at least five perpetrators, but as of yet, no explanation has been given as to why these people were attacked. However, we do know that all of the known suspects were killed by the police when they arrived."

"Was there a shootout?"

"From what I have been told, no, there was no exchange of gunfire between the alleged killers and the police."

"Can you tell us why the police decided to use deadly force?"

"Well, Tom, from what Sergeant Harrison has stated to the press, when the police arrived on the scene, the alleged killers—a group of four males and one female—were observed to be eating their victims."

"Eating, you say?"

"Yes, Tom, that's correct. Several witnesses also reported that some of the victims were eaten alive in an apparent act of cannibalism. Some of the witnesses have stated that the victims were bitten and torn apart by their killers. However, this has not been confirmed by the authorities as of yet. The bodies have been turned over to the coroner and will await autopsy."

"Carol, do we know how many people were killed?"

"Well, Tom, there are at least nine confirmed deaths and seven injured, but at the moment it is still unclear just how many were actually were killed in the attack."

"Thank you, Carol. We'll check back with you later as more news develops."

"Thanks, Tom."

"This is Tom Reynolds, and you're listening to 88.9 FM, WFSU radio—bringing you the latest breaking news in Tallahassee.

"For those of you just joining us: there has been a string of mass murders in Leon County and surrounding areas. Numerous reports of violent crimes continue to pour in from all areas of the city. Authorities are asking citizens to remain indoors until further notice.

"We have also been receiving nationwide reports of similar activity from various sources. Television and Internet services remain down throughout the city and surrounding areas at the time of this broadcast. Some areas are reported to be without power.

"We will continue to keep you informed on these and other stories as more information is received."

The broadcast ended abruptly as static blasted from the radio's speakers. Samantha Adams sat motionless in her little Honda Civic, staring blankly at the road ahead. Her long, dark hair flapped wildly in the wind from the open sunroof as she drove down the old, familiar road. Slowly, she turned down the volume on the radio and the loud static subsided. She tuned the dial, scanning for other stations, but there were no other broadcasts; at least none that she could pick up on the rural countryside. Usually, she was able to pick up most of the Tallahassee stations from this location, but now only the crackling drone of static could be heard. Strange indeed, she thought to herself.

She reflected on the disturbing news that had just played on the radio. It seemed surreal. She almost couldn't believe what she had just heard. Only twenty minutes had passed since she left Florida State University. Everything had seemed normal—except for the attendance. Before her classes, she was actually able to find a parking space on time—a rare occurrence at the overpopulated college. A lot of students had been absent that day. But it was Friday, Samantha reminded herself. She had witnessed nothing out of the ordinary.

The bizarre radio announcement replayed again in the young woman's mind. She tensed up as she thought about her boyfriend. He usually got off work early on Fridays, but she feared for his safety. She hoped to God that he had made it home okay. She pressed on the gas, increasing her speed to seventy miles-per-hour along the old country road as she headed toward the little trailer in the woods.

Samantha lived with her boyfriend on an old dirt road way out in the sticks, and she loved the privacy. The only thing she didn't like about it was the inconvenience of having to drive thirty miles just to get groceries. Both she and her boyfriend had to make the long drive to the city almost every day.

Her boyfriend was a typical country-boy. He had grown up in a rural town outside Tallahassee, and his father was a sportsman. His father had taken him hunting and fishing from an early age on. He was a simple, hard-working young man who cared little for the big city. He worked happily as a mechanic at a small garage just outside the city-limits. He had no desire to go to college, but he admired Samantha for pursuing her dreams.

Samantha wanted to be a college professor when she finished school. She was in her junior year as a psychology major. She loved nothing more than to study and analyze human behavior.

As she neared the little dirt road, she put on her turn signal. Slowing down at the stop sign, she noticed a hunched-over elderly lady walking slowly alongside the dusty road. The woman was dressed light-blue nightgown and she had curlers in her hair. A pair of black, horn-rimmed glasses rested loosely on her nose. Drawing closer, Samantha recognized the little old lady—it was Mrs. Thompson, an Alzheimer's patient who lived down the road. The young woman pulled up beside her, rolling down the passenger-side window.

"Hi Missus Thompson," Samantha said, putting the car in neutral. "Do you need a ride?"

The old woman turned to face the car, her frail body moving sluggishly with age. Her wrinkled skin was as pale as a ghost, and her eyes looked sickly. As the woman approached the car, she tripped suddenly on a fallen branch, hitting her head into the metal door.

"Missus Thompson!" the young woman cried, unbuckling her seatbelt. She jumped out of the car, leaving the engine on as she rushed around to the other side of the vehicle.

The old woman lay sprawled out in the sand at the edge of the dusty road. Samantha helped her up, opening the passenger door.

"Let's get you home," the young woman said, helping the elderly woman into the seat.

The old woman slouched back in the passenger's seat, moaning as Samantha got back into the car.

"You all right?" the young woman asked, putting the car into gear as she pressed on the gas. The car drove off down the sandy road, a loud of dust trailing behind.

Suddenly, the old woman grabbed Samantha's right arm and pulled it toward her mouth. She snarled, her mouth wide-open, as she leaned across the seat toward the young woman.

Samantha let out a high-pitched scream, yanking her arm away from the old lady's grasp. Startled, she leaned back against the window, taking her hands off the steering wheel. The car careened off the road, narrowly missing a pine tree.

The hunchbacked woman reached out again, clawing wildly at the younger woman's face as the vehicle sped out of control though the forest.

With a loud crash, the car collided head-on into a large oak tree as the windshield shattered into pieces. The force of the sudden crash lifted the rear of the small car into the air, slamming back down into the ground violently. The slow-moving vehicle rolled back a few feet before coming to a stop.

Samantha sat motionless for a moment as she caught her breath. The driver's airbag had blown up in her face and for a moment she wasn't sure what had happened. Then she looked over at the passenger seat, realizing that Mrs. Thompson had been ejected out of the car through the windshield.

Samantha took a deep breath and unbuckled her seatbelt. She pushed against the door and the car shook as it swung open with a creaking noise, causing an avalanche of glass to fall from the shattered windshield.

As she stumbled out into the thicket, she noticed that the hood of the car was smashed in completely. She surveyed the damage as she walked around the large oak. Shattered glass crunched beneath her shoes as she moved. About ten feet in front of the tree, the old woman was laying face-down on the ground.

"Missus Thompson?" Samantha gasped as she approached the motionless body. She knelt down on the grass to get a closer look. The old woman's neck was twisted awkwardly to one side. Her eyes were open, staring vacantly off into space.

Suddenly, the old woman's eyes jerked, fixing their steady gaze on the younger woman.

Samantha fell backward in shock and landed on her back. She rolled over to her side, catching a glimpse as the elderly woman as she stood up, her neck hanging ineptly to one side.

The old lady lurched forward, a horrible gurgling sound escaping from her open mouth as she moved. She tumbled onto Samantha as she lay on the ground stunned with fright.

The two women struggled on the ground, rolling around in the dirt. The older woman clawed wildly at Samantha, but her fragile body was no match for the younger woman's strength. As the old woman opened her mouth and snapped her teeth ferociously, Samantha slammed a fist into her jaw. The old woman's dentures flew out of her mouth in a trail of slobber as her neck snapped to one side with a loud crack.

Samantha shoved the old woman off of her, and jumped up quickly to her feet. She backed away slowly, keeping her eyes firmly locked on the hideous old woman. The lady's neck was now contorted into a dreadfully awkward position, her head hanging down limply. Her eyes rolled up into her head as she tried in vain to look up. Drool poured out in strings from her toothless mouth as she snarled viciously at the younger woman, stumbling forward.

The ghastly woman lurched forward, and Samantha lost her footing as she stepped back, falling helplessly onto the contorted hood of the car. The atrocious old woman lunged forward again, just as Samantha rolled off the hood onto the ground. The older woman tumbled face-down onto the hood.

Samantha jumped up, sprinting away through the trees without looking back. She ran as fast as her legs would carry her toward the dirt road. When reached the road, she turned and kept running as her heart pounded rapidly in her chest. In the distance ahead of her on the side of the road, she saw a metal object reflecting sunlight. As she approached the glaring object, she saw that it was a silver-colored mailbox, which she instantly recognized. It belonged to her neighbors, an older retired couple, who were usually home during the daytime. She slowed down as she approached her neighbor's dirt driveway, where she caught sight of a man walking down the wooded path toward the road.

"Help!" Samantha cried, running toward the approaching figure with her arms waving wildly at her sides. She felt a sense of relief when she recognized the man. It was her neighbor, Mr. Gardner, the older retired man. She slowed her pace to a brisk walk as she approached him, and he paused for a moment when her saw her. She was glad she had seen him when she did—he usually walked to his mailbox around this time of day to get his mail.

"You'll never believe what just happened," Samantha said, her voice trembling as she spoke.

The old man stared blankly at her for a few moments, and then walked toward her. He uttered a strange moaning sound as he stumbled awkwardly toward her.

"Mister Gardner?" Samantha gasped, coming to an abrupt stop. She backed away slowly as the old man continued to limp forward, reaching out his arms as if to grab her. As he got closer to her, she noticed a large open wound on the side of man's neck, which was bleeding profusely onto his blue and white flannel shirt. Her mouth dropped open in surprise, unable to utter a word out of sheer fright. She wanted to scream, but not even a sound could escape her throat. Terrified for her life once again, she turned and ran back to the road without even looking back. This time, she headed straight for her little trailer in the woods, which she knew would be a ways further down the road.

After about a mile of running, she came to a stop, catching her breath. She looked over her shoulder at the road behind her. No one was in sight. The road was empty except for the small trail of dust that she had kicked up. She looked back to the road ahead, spotting her mailbox in the distance. She rested for a moment, taking deep breaths before jogging off toward the driveway. As she approached the familiar green trailer, she saw her boyfriend's brown pickup truck in the front yard. She breathed a sigh of relief and rushed up the little staircase onto the wooden porch.

"Charlie!" she cried, banging on the screen door as tears streamed down her cheeks. "Open up!"

# 3

Mark awoke to the smell of bacon and eggs. He lay on the couch for a few minutes, staring sleepily at the ceiling as he fought the urge to go back to sleep. He looked up at the clock. It was 8:12 AM. He sat up and looked around the room. Luke, Joe and Sean were sound asleep on the floor. The recliner where Scott had been sitting the night before was empty, but the shotgun was leaning against the back of the chair. The radio was still on, but only static came from the speakers.

Mark stood up and stretched his arms, yawning. He grabbed the handgun from the end table and tucked it into the back of his jeans. He walked through the dining room into the kitchen, and the sounds of grease sizzling in a pan became audible as he entered the room.

Scott was standing in front of the stove with a spatula in one hand and a cigarette dangling from his mouth. He was shirtless, revealing the various tattoos on his shoulders and arms. Pots and pans littered the kitchen counter, and one of the pans was full of freshly cooked bacon strips.

"Morning," Scott said without looking up. He took a deep drag from his cigarette and flipped over some eggs in a pan. "You hungry?"

Mark scratched the back of his neck and leaned against the counter.

"I'm starved."

Scott grabbed a paper plate from a cabinet and slapped a serving of eggs on it. "Help yourself," he insisted, exhaling a cloud of smoke as he handed the plate to his brother.

Mark took the plate of eggs and put a couple of pieces of bacon on it. He walked into the dining room and sat at the table, which faced a large window framed with tall, purple curtains.

"That's the last of the eggs," Scott said. "So enjoy them while you can."

"Something smells good," a sleepy-sounding voice said from the living room.

Mark looked up and saw Joe walking into the room, rubbing his eyes.

"Morning, Joe," Mark said. "How did you sleep?"

"Okay, I guess," Joe replied, yawning. "But I've got one hell of a hangover." He walked into the kitchen and filled a glass with water, and gulped it down as he walked back into the dining room.

Scott followed Joe into the dining room and placed a plate full of eggs and bacon strips on the table. "Grab a plate," he told Joe as he put his cigarette out in an ashtray, and made himself a plate. Joe took a plate and the two men joined Mark at the table. They sat quietly for a few minutes eating their breakfast.

Then Scott broke the silence. "So," he said, chewing on a piece of bacon. "Did you guys hear the news this morning?"

Joe shook his head with his mouth full.

"I must have been asleep," Mark replied. "What happened?

"Well they went off the air around two AM," Scott said. "But they came back on around four." He paused to take a bite of his eggs, and then continued. "They said some people were reporting crazy things like alien sightings and dead people getting up and walking. Crazy shit like that."

Joe laughed, spitting pieces of egg on his plate. "Aliens?" he said, chuckling. "What were those people smoking? And walking dead people? What's up with that?"

Mark stopped eating for a moment and looked over at Scott.

"Yeah," Scott said. "I think everybody's gone mad. There are fucking cannibals out there, and a lot of people are gettin' killed. And now people are seein' shit. I wanna know what the hell's goin' on!"

"That's crazy!" Mark exclaimed. "What if terrorists put acid in the water system or something? Everybody's freaking out!"

Suddenly, a loud banging noise came from the kitchen door.

"What the hell is that?" Joe said, dropping his fork.

Mark stood up quickly, retrieved his handgun from his jeans, and cocked it. "Stay here, I'll go check." He walked cautiously into the kitchen, holding the gun with both hands.

Scott jumped up and disappeared into the living room for a few seconds, and then returned carrying his shotgun. The banging sound continued.

After a minute or two, Mark rushed back into the dining room, wide-eyed and breathing heavily. "You're not gonna believe this," he said anxiously.

"What?" Scott yelled.

"It's that cop…" Mark said with a gulp, "the one from last night!"

Joe jumped up out of his chair, knocking his plate off the table with a loud crash.

Five seconds later, Sean and Luke burst into the room, eyes half shut.

"What's going on?" Luke demanded in a hoarse, sleepy voice as he put on his glasses.

Mark looked at Sean. "The cop that tried to attack us last night is at the door!" he exclaimed.

"Shit!" Sean yelled.

"Everybody be quiet!" Scott ordered, raising the shotgun with one hand. He made a motion with his other hand, signaling for the others to get down. He knelt down against the wall, hiding from the view of the dining room window. The other four men crouched down where they were standing.

The banging continued, growing louder and louder.

"What do you think he wants?" Luke asked softly, pushing his glasses up with his index finger.

"I'm pretty sure he wants to kill us!" Mark whispered angrily.

The five men huddled in the dining room for several minutes as the banging continued. Then, it suddenly stopped and the house was quiet. The young men looked at each other, but didn't say a word for fear that the police officer would hear them.

Suddenly, the dining room window smashed open with a loud crash, sending shards of glass flying into the room.

Luke let out a high-pitched scream and jumped backward as Scott pumped his shotgun and stood up quickly, facing the window.

A woman with long, frizzy blonde hair stood at the broken window, clawing at the remaining shards of glass protruding from the around the window. Her skin was extremely pale, and her eyes were as white as snow.

As Scott stood staring at the growling woman, the other four men crawled away from the dining room into the kitchen. Once in the kitchen, Mark remained kneeling at the doorway to the dining room and aimed his pistol at the female in the window.

"What the hell do you want?" Scott demanded, as he aimed his shotgun firmly at the wild-haired woman's chest.

The woman ignored him and continued snarling like an animal as she clawed at the remaining glass in the window frame, sending pieces of broken glass shattering to the floor.

"Back off, bitch!" Scott warned, and he poked the woman with the barrel of his shotgun

The woman swung one of her arms, clawing violently at Scott, and lost her balance. She fell head-first through the window onto her belly, and immediately looked up at the man pointing the shotgun at her. She began crawling toward him through the broken glass, baring her teeth as she growled. Her milky-white eyes blazed at him, and she left little droplets of blood on the white floor as her hands and knees crunched into the shards of glass.

Scott fired a deafening blast from the shotgun, striking the woman directly in the crown of her head at close-range. Her skull exploded, splattering brain and bone fragments in all directions. The nearby walls and furniture were drenched in blood as her body crumpled lifelessly to the wooden floor.

Scott cocked his shotgun, ejecting the empty shell as a wisp of smoke rose from the chamber.

"Jesus Christ!" Joe exclaimed, wide-eyed with terror.

An eerie silence crept into the room as the spent shell hit the floor with a tapping sound, and rolled to a stop. The young men stood motionless for a moment, staring in disbelief at the gory spectacle before them. Time seemed to stand still for a moment for the young men as they scanned the room.

Scott walked to the broken window as glass fragments crunched under his feet. He leaned one foot against the windowsill and stuck his head out cautiously. He glanced quickly in both directions, and ducked back inside.

Suddenly, the banging sound came again from the front kitchen door. In unison, the five young men turned their attention to the kitchen.

"For Christ's sake!" Mark exclaimed, stomping furiously toward the carport door.

When he reached the door, he saw the uniformed officer banging on the small window with open hands. The bite wound from the night before was still visible on the man's neck. Dried blood was caked all over his shirt, and the flesh on his face had turned a bluish-gray color.

Suddenly, Mark smashed the door open with a swift kick, knocking the officer off the front stairs. The man's body crashed down onto the hard concrete in the carport. As he landed, his legs bent up, revealing his torn pants leg and shredded flesh where he had been bitten the night before.

"What the *hell* is wrong with you people?" Mark yelled angrily, aiming the Glock wildly at the man.

The officer stood up slowly, his milky white eyes blazing at the big man. He let out a loud, horrible groan, and started walking toward Mark. His stiff, bloody arms reached out as if to grab him.

"You dumb bastard!" Mark roared, and fired two consecutive shots into the man's chest. The empty shells that ejected from the pistol clinked on the concrete and rolled around.

The officer staggered back as the bullets pierced his ribcage, spilling fresh blood onto his tattered uniform. He wobbled around on his injured leg, moaning. Then he walked toward Mark again, his mouth wide open as he groaned hoarsely.

Mark took several steps back. "Die!" he yelled, and he pointed the Glock at the policeman again. He fired another round, but missed completely.

Suddenly, Scott emerged from the doorway and grabbed Mark's wrist.

"Save your ammo," Scott told him.

Scott lifted his shotgun and aimed it carefully at the crazy, uniformed man. As soon as the officer walked within range, he fired a loud shot into the man's chest, sending him soaring backward into the air. The man landed flat on his back. His legs twitched for a moment, and then his body lay motionless.

"Nice shot," Mark said, patting his brother on the back.

Scott cocked the shotgun, expelling the spent shell and loading another. He hesitated for a few seconds, gazing intently at the motionless body of the fallen deputy. Then he walked cautiously toward it as his brother followed closely behind.

They stood over the body, which was oozing dark blood from its mouth and nostrils. Its shirt was now shredded to pieces and drenched in thick blood from the gunshot wounds.

Suddenly, the officer's eyes sprung open.

The two brothers jumped back in shock.

The fatally wounded man lay motionless for a moment, his pale, sickly eyes staring up at the sky.

Then, his horrid gaze fixed abruptly on the two men that had shot him. A deathly wail escaped from his open mouth as he slowly sat up. Dark blood gushed from his nose, running down his lips and chin.

"Holy shit!" Mark cried, grimacing behind his brother.

Scott blasted another deafening shot at the gruesome-looking man. The discharge caught him in the kidneys, thrusting him over on his side.

Slowly, the man sat back up as his entrails spilled out onto the concrete. Blood trickled off of his chin as he cocked his head back. He growled loudly, gurgling blood in his throat and lungs.

Mark looked fearfully at his brother. "Shoot it, man! Shoot it again!"

Scott pumped the shotgun and walked up to the gory, blood-drenched deputy. He aimed carefully at his head as the man reached out awkwardly, trying to grab at him.

"How the hell is he still alive?" Mark yelled frantically.

Scott aimed the barrel of the shotgun point-blank at the officer's face. He let loose an earsplitting blast, and the man's skull burst open, spewing bright red blood into the air. The decapitated corpse dropped flaccidly to the ground. Thick blood flowed out from its neck and collected into puddles around the body.

"He's dead *now*," Scott announced as he grabbed a handful of shotgun shells from his pocket.

The two young men stood over the corpse of the policeman for a few moments while Scott loaded four more shells into the gun. Then they walked back toward the house.

"Behind you!" a voiced called from the kitchen door. Luke, Joe and Sean had been standing in the doorway, observing the gruesome spectacle from a distance.

The two brothers turned around and spotted two people approaching from the road. The distant figures wobbled stiffly with their arms stretched outward as they walked down the driveway.

"Let's get inside," Mark advised as he pressed lightly against his brother's back, urging him back toward the door.

Scott stood staring at the two figures in the distance for a minute, and then followed his brother into the carport. As he walked, he spotted a stack of plywood, which was leaning against a corner of the house. He quickly picked up a piece of the wood.

"Grab a hammer and some nails," he instructed Mark as he walked up the steps into the kitchen.

Mark rushed over to a tool chest in the carport and retrieved two hammers. He searched through the drawers until he found a bag of nails. As he walked toward the door, he noticed a machete leaning against the wall, and picked it up. Then he dashed up stairs into the kitchen, and Joe slammed the door shut and locked the bolt. He handed Joe a hammer, while Luke eagerly grabbed the machete.

Scott called them together into the dining room, where he had leaned the piece of plywood against a wall. "Give me a hand with this," he said, grabbing the dead woman's body by the ankles.

Joe grasped the body by its wrists as he cringed in disgust. They lifted the corpse and carried it to the broken window.

"On three," Scott said, and they swung it back and forth. "One...two...*three!*" They let go of the dead body, hurling it through the window onto the front porch.

"Here they come!" Mark yelled from the kitchen as he peered out through the small glass window on the door.

Scott grabbed the piece of plywood and pressed it firmly against the window. Mark rushed into the room and retrieved a handful of nails from the bag. Scott held the wood against the window as Mark and Joe nailed it to the wall.

Once the window was boarded up, Mark ran back into the kitchen and gazed out through the window on the door.

"I don't see 'em!" he exclaimed, peering out from different angles.

Suddenly, a loud thumping noise came from the front of the house.

"They're on the front porch!" Sean yelled from the dining room.

The five men rushed into the living room. They spotted the shadows of two moving figures through the curtains. The shadowy figures' feet thudded against the wooden deck as they stumbled around outside.

"I'm going to try nine-one-one again," Luke said as he ran down the hall. He hurried into the bedroom and picked up the phone, but the line was dead. "Shit!" he cried, and rushed back into the living room.

Joe noticed that the radio was broadcasting again, so he turned up the volume as the two people bumped around on the front porch.

"*...it is unlikely that the attacks will cease anytime soon if our theories are correct. Their numbers will continue to grow in* *exponential proportions as their victims will inevitably join them.*

*"If you are just joining us, we are talking with Doctor Richard H. Johnson of Florida State University about the sudden outbreak of violent attacks, murders, and cannibalism.*

*"A group of scientists and government authorities have come to the conclusion that the recent dead are returning to life and attacking the living."*

"What the hell?" Scott gasped, clenching his shotgun tightly.

"Jesus!" Luke exclaimed. "No fucking way!"

Joe leaned over the radio and turned up the volume.

*"Authorities had previously instructed various news agencies to advise the public to remain in their homes with the doors locked. However, we've recently received word of conflicting reports.*

*"A martial law has been placed into effect for Leon county and surrounding areas. All citizens are instructed to move to local emergency shelters by nightfall. The National Guard has been called in to assist with the evacuation of heavily populated areas.*

*"We'll have a list of these emergency rescue stations within the next hour."*

Suddenly, the front window smashed open, hurling pieces of glass onto the living room floor. Four arms reached through the broken window, flailing around, as if to grab something or someone. The arms poked in and out of the curtains.

Luke swung his machete impulsively at one of the arms and chopped it off. It snapped off just above the elbow, and the severed limb flew through the air, landing on the carpet. The detached arm twitched and jerked as blood spurted out onto the carpet.

Mark pulled the curtains back away from the window, revealing a tall, skinny man with dark curly hair. Beside him stood a short, fat man with a bald head, and curly white hair on the sides of his head. The fat man was shirtless, sporting only a pair of cut-off shorts. The skinny man wore a black suit, and looked as if he was dressed for a funeral. The skinny man was also missing his left arm. Their skin was pale and bluish, and their eyes were vacant and white.

"If the radio's right," Scott said, noting the way the men wobbled around clumsily, "then these guys are walking corpses!"

"Shoot 'em!" Joe yelled.

"How do you kill 'em if they're already dead?" Mark cried, pointing his handgun at the window.

"Shooting them in the head seems to work," Scott replied.

Mark walked closer to the window and aimed his Glock at the skinny, one-armed man's forehead. The man tried in vain to grab him with his only arm, reaching out awkwardly through the window. Mark fired a single shot directly between the man's eyes, and he slumped limply over the windowsill.

Suddenly, the fat man grabbed Mark's arm, trying to bite it. Mark tried to pull away but the fat man gripped onto him tightly with both hands.

Scott cocked his shotgun and pressed the barrel against the bald man's ear. He fired a loud blast directly into the man's head, and it splattered into an explosion of blood and skull fragments.

Mark covered his ears as the shotgun blast rang out, and drops of blood spattered into his face and shirt.

The fat man's body clung lifelessly to Mark's shirt for a moment. Then he pushed it back with a powerful shove, sending it slamming down onto the wooden deck with a loud thud.

"This is insane!" Luke exclaimed as he held the blood-splattered machete up in one hand.

Sean walked up to the skinny man's body which was slumped over the windowsill and pushed it out onto the porch. All the while, the radio continued to broadcast.

*"...I repeat: it is unsafe to remain in your home, no matter how well-armed or prepared you think you may be.*

*"State and local authorities have issued a new mandate. Citizens may no longer remain in private residences and must report to the specially-designated rescue station nearest their location. Please listen for the emergency rescue station nearest you:*

*"Leon High School, East Tennessee Street; Tallahassee Police Department Headquarters, Seventh Avenue; Tallahassee Community College, Appleyard Drive; First Baptist Church, West College Avenue; Tallahassee Memorial Hospital, Miccosukee Road..."*

"We've got to get to one of those shelters," Luke insisted as he scratched his beard nervously.

"I'm not going back out there!" Joe exclaimed.

"Our families are probably at some of those stations!"

"And what if they're not?"

"We'll take our chances," Scott butted in.

"Oh, no we won't!" Mark exclaimed. "We'll be here, as long as we keep those creeps out there and we stay in here."

"What about the *radio*?" Luke cried.

"Fuck the radio," Mark retorted.

"Mark's right," Sean broke in. "It's too risky to leave right now."

"Holy shit!" Joe yelled, pointing out the front windows.

Three more creatures were walking slowly toward the house from the main road.

"Grab some more plywood!" Scott advised. "We need to board up those windows!"

The five young men dashed into the kitchen and unlocked the door. They hurried over to the stack of boards, and each of them grabbed a piece of plywood. Once they got back inside, they bolted the lock back into place.

"Hurry," Mark urged, breathing heavily as they ran back into the living room.

The three zombies were about thirty yards from the house by the time the five men reached the broken windows. Sean held a board against one window and Luke covered the other window. Mark and Joe began nailing them to the wall as Scott handed them nails.

As soon as the last nail was pounded into place, the banging started from outside. The three creatures had climbed onto the porch and were pushing and clawing against the wooden barriers, but they held up against the attacks.

"We should secure the windows in the back too," Luke suggested, fearful that more zombies would come and try to break through. He dragged a piece of plywood over to the other side of the room, where two windows faced the backyard. The other young men helped him board up the windows securely.

The banging and scratching noises continued from the front porch, growing louder over the next hour as more zombies began to show up. As expected, the noises also started coming from the back windows and the dining room, eventually surrounding the house with a barrage of thrashing and pounding sounds. The five men spread out, reinforcing the boarded-up windows as the invaders banged against the wood.

Eventually, Scott decided it was time to add additional protection, and he started boarding up the smaller windows, such as the ones on the doors and the little window above the kitchen sink.

The other four young men moved furniture such as bookcases, tables, and chairs against the windows for added support.

"We should be okay for a while," Mark said as sweat trickled down his brow. "As long as we can keep the windows reinforced, and as long as we have food and running water, we should be able to hold out."

The five young men stood quietly for a few minutes listening to the banging, scratching, and moaning sounds that were coming from outside. They finished off the food that Scott had cooked while the sounds continued. After several hours had passed, they began to get used to the racket.

They sat around listening to the radio announcements, and reinforcing the boarded-up windows as the need arose.

Charlie had been listening to the radio all afternoon until the signal had abruptly cut off. At first, he thought the strange news reports were some kind of sick joke. But it wasn't long before the crazy people began to show up outside the little trailer. He warned them to go away when they started beating on the walls, but they just wouldn't respond. It was as if they had lost their minds and couldn't speak. He had tried to call the police, but strangely, there was no phone service either. He locked the doors and tried to put up with the relentless noise, but they just wouldn't stop. Finally, after two hours of total madness, he decided to go outside and give them a good beating. He was, after all, twice their size. A good ass-whooping would teach the bastards a lesson, he thought—that was, until they tried to bite him. That was the last straw. He gave them a final warning as he pushed them away, but they continued to come after him. They even broke one of the windows when he went back inside to get his hunting rifle.

He went back out on the porch, figuring they would run off when they saw his gun. But to the contrary—they clawed at him and tried to bite him again. He remembered the radio announcements about the mass murder taking place in the city—and the crazy reports of cannibalism—and something suddenly clicked in his head. He now realized that they wouldn't stop until they killed him.

As he stood staring in horror at the ghastly figures before him, one of the people—a middle-aged man with a receding hairline and a mustache—tackled him down onto the wooden porch. Charlie quickly pushed him off with a powerful shove, and fired the rifle into the man's stomach. But the shot didn't even faze the madman, and he continued to creep toward Charlie. He fired again, putting a bullet through the man's skull, and this time he stopped moving.

*It was self-defense*, Charlie thought to himself. These people were crazy—they were trying to kill him in his own home. As the other people advanced steadily toward him, he fired again and again, putting a bullet in each of their heads as they fell one by one. He waited with his rifle still poised, eyeing the bodies curiously for several minutes before walking back inside.

As he sat in the little green trailer with the doors locked, the big, muscular man began to worry about his girlfriend. She was supposed to be home already. He waited another thirty minutes, and two more of the crazy people showed up in the back yard. He watched them curiously from the bedroom window, noticing their unusually pale skin tones. One of them even had a knife protruding from the back of his flannel shirt. The man's wound was still dripping blood, but he moved about as if he didn't even notice it was there.

A loud knock came from the front door. Startled, Charlie jumped up, his heart pounding in his chest. He stood still for a few moments as the banging continued, growing louder with each passing second. He grabbed his rifle and walked quickly into the living room. The knocking became more intense as he drew closer to the door. He could see the silhouette of a woman through the white curtains on the door window. He placed the barrel of the rifle up to the outline of the figure's head and put his finger on the trigger.

"Charlie!" a female voice shouted frantically from the other side of the door. "Open up!"

The big man instantly recognized the familiar voice and unlocked the door. He swung the door open and Samantha burst through, falling into the big man's arms with tears in her eyes.

"Samantha!" the husky man cried, shutting the door behind her. "Thank God you're all right!" He quickly turned the lock on the door back into place and dropped the rifle at his side. Then he turned and hugged the small-framed young woman tightly in his massive arms.

Samantha couldn't get the words out. She was frightened out of her mind, yet she was filled with relief as the big man hugged her. She felt so protected in his arms.

"You *are* all right," Charlie asked as he wiped the young woman's tears from her eyes, "aren't you?"

"Missus Thompson..." she struggled to get the words out.

"What?" the big man asked.

"Missus Thompson from down the road," Samantha gasped. "She attacked me and..." Her voice trailed off.

"It's okay, honey. Go on."

"We crashed. We crashed into a tree and...and I think she was dead!"

"She died?"

"No...she was *already dead!*" The young woman looked Charlie in the eyes with a strange frown on her face.

"It's okay, sweetie. I know. Something terrible is going out there. I've heard the news." He gave her a reassuring look as he held her close in his arms.

"I was listening, too. I can't believe it. I just can't believe..."

Suddenly, the window on the door shattered behind the young couple. They quickly spun around to see a long, bloody arm reaching out at them through the broken glass.

"Get away from the door, Samantha!" Charlie yelled as he scooped up his rifle. He pushed the barrel through the curtains on the door as the bloody hand grabbed onto the black metal. A horrible moaning sound came from behind the door as the bloody hand tugged at the gun. When he felt the tip of the barrel hit the nose of the figure behind the curtains, he squeezed the trigger. The rifle fired a loud blast, and the moaning came to an abrupt stop. The blood-covered arm loosened its grip on the barrel of the gun and slid back through the window. A loud thump came from behind the door as the body collapsed on the wooden porch.

Samantha gave her brawny boyfriend another big hug and the couple backed away from the door into the living room.

"We'll have to do something about those windows," Charlie said. He sat down on the coffee table and rested the rifle across his lap. "Those…*things*…won't be able to get in if we board 'em up good enough."

Samantha sat down beside the big man. "Do we still have all that wood in the utility closet?"

"Yeah, it's still there," Charlie said, gazing at the curtains on the door as they fluttered about in the cool breeze. He grabbed a bag of nails and two hammers from the closet, and gave one of the hammers to Samantha. Then he brought some of the small boards and pieces of plywood into the living room and stacked them into a small pile.

"I can't believe we're doing this," Samantha said as she picked up a piece of wood and nailed it across one of the windows above the couch.

"Don't worry," Charlie assured her. "Everything's going to be just fine."

As soon as he finished speaking, a loud crash erupted from the bedroom at the end of the hall. Charlie rushed down the narrow hallway with his rifle, and Samantha followed closely behind. As they reached the doorway to the bedroom, they saw that the carpet was covered in shattered glass. One of the windows next to the bed was broken, and a pale-looking man with a mustache was leaning halfway through the window. His arms flailed around wildly, spattering small drops of blood around the room from the open wounds on his forearms. The man snarled at the young couple when he saw them, and drool oozed from his open mouth onto the carpet.

"Don't look at it!" Charlie said. "Hurry and get me a big piece of plywood. I'll take care of it." He watched as Samantha raced back down the hallway, her heart pounding in her chest as she ran. As soon as he saw her reach the living room, he walked over to the window and grabbed the horrid creature by its thin, gray hair, and lifted its head up. A grotesque gurgling sound escaped from its mouth as he yanked it backward in a quick motion, snapping its neck back. The creature slid back through the window, but its chin got caught on the bottom of the window sill. Although its neck appeared to be broken, it still growled and snapped its teeth, with its gaze fixed firmly on the large man standing over it. Charlie shook his head in disgust, and pressed the barrel of his rifle against the creature's forehead. He pulled the trigger, and a bullet smashed through the ghoul's head, exiting at the base of its skull in a spurt of blood and grey matter.

"I got it," Samantha said from the doorway. She stared in horror at the gruesome, blood-covered body in the window frame. Holding back a wave of nausea, she handed a large piece of plywood to Charlie.

The big man nodded and took the board from Samantha. He kicked the lifeless corpse in the head with the heel of his boot, and the body slid outside onto the ground. He stuck his head out through the broken window and scanned the yard for any more of the creatures. There were two of them in view of the window, but neither of them was close enough to pose any immediate danger. He ducked back inside and pressed the large piece of wood against the window frame. Samantha helped him nail it to the wall.

"This should hold," Charlie said as he nailed a final nail into the corner of the board. "I'd rather be safe than sorry, though." He walked over to the large oak dresser and scooped up the various items that rested on it, tossing them onto the bed in one swift motion. Then he pushed the dresser across the room, sliding it against the boarded-up window for extra support.

"Charlie, I'm scared," Samantha said, folding her arms nervously against her chest as she rocked slowly back and forth.

"We'll be all right in here," the big man said in a comforting tone. "More of them will come, but I don't think they'll be able to get in. We should be safe until…"

"Until what?" Samantha asked, cutting him off.

"Until…" Charlie paused for a moment, his voice trailing off. "Until help arrives."

"Oh, Charlie," the young woman said, as tears welled up in her eyes. She rushed over to her boyfriend and fell into his arms, embracing him tightly. "Do you think they'll really come?"

"Yes," Charlie replied without a second thought. "I'm sure of it."

By the sixth day of holing up in the Walkers' two-story house, the five young men were as safe as they could be in their boarded-up fortress. No zombies had gotten through their barriers. They had worked very hard, using every resource available to reinforce the blockades on the windows. They had even taken down doors from the interior of the house and nailed them to the walls.

They had kept themselves busy during the week playing every board game the Walkers owned—including chess, checkers, Monopoly, and Scrabble. They had listened to the radio constantly, keeping up to date on the news and the status of the emergency rescue stations. A couple of the stations had reportedly been shut down after being overrun by hordes of the walking dead.

The five men would have had it made, had it not been for one small factor—they were running out of food, and fast!

"The time has come for us to move on," Mark said as he stood in front of the T.V., which had been broadcasting the same static and snow for the past week. "We have to get to one of those rescue stations!"

"I'm not going out *there*," Luke said, shaking his head. "Not with those *things* out there."

"We'd have to be crazy to leave now!" Joe exclaimed. "Those creatures will tear us apart!"

"I know it's dangerous out there," Mark replied. "But we're just going to have to risk it. If we can make it to Leon High, we should be safe."

"How the hell are we gonna get past those things?" Sean asked, bewildered.

"We'd have to work together," Scott broke in.

"There's no way, man!" Luke exclaimed.

"We have no other choice," Mark said, matter-of-factly. "It's either stay in here and starve to death, or go out there and risk being eaten alive. But at least we'd have a chance at surviving!"

"He's right," Sean added. "If we stay here, we won't last much longer. I for one would rather die trying than to give up and die of hunger!"

"And what if our car was to break down," Luke hypothesized, "or get a flat tire? There are many things that could go wrong."

"Those are risks we'll have to have to take," Scott said.

"And that's why we need a plan," Mark added. "If we take two vehicles—Sean's van and Scott's car—then we would have a backup. If something happened to one of them, we'd still have the other."

"Good idea," Scott affirmed.

"But how are we going to even get to the cars?" Luke asked. "The yard is crawling with those creatures."

"You're right," Mark agreed. "There are quite a few of them out there now, but they're pretty slow. They're not really any match for our speed. We can outrun 'em easily."

"And Mark and I can provide covering fire," Scott added. "It shouldn't be that hard to get around them."

"I guess you're right," Joe sighed. "When do we leave?"

"Let's all pack up anything we think we may need," Mark said. "I think we should leave first thing in the morning so that we'll have the maximum amount of daylight."

"Good thinking," Sean said. "I'll check upstairs for anything that we might be able use on the trip."

"All right," Mark concurred. "Joe, come help me gather up the remaining food."

"I guess Luke and I will start packing up the rest of the stuff," Scott said, and Luke nodded his head in agreement.

The five men used the rest of the day to gather up supplies and to prepare to leave the next day.

The next morning, the men woke to the loud buzzing of Scott's alarm clock at 7:00 AM.

Luke got up and walked to the boarded up living room windows and peeked through a crack in the plywood. For a moment, the bright morning sunlight was all he could see.

Suddenly, a hand slammed into the wood, causing Luke to jump back in surprise. A gray-skinned man with white eyes clawed at the boards on the front porch.

"They're still out there," Luke said as his heart raced from the shock. He pushed his plastic-rimmed glasses up on his nose and backed away from the windows.

"Don't worry about 'em," Scott told Luke. "Just grab your stuff and let's get on the road."

"You're ready to go already?" Sean asked.

"The earlier we leave," Scott replied. "The more daylight we'll have. I don't want to get stranded out there after dark."

"You have a point."

The five friends grabbed their belongings and walked into the kitchen, gathering around the door to the carport. Scott's silver two-door car was parked in the carport, and Sean's van was in the driveway. A black zombie with an afro was pressing its face against the window on the kitchen door, as if it were trying to walk through the glass.

"How are we gonna to do this?" Mark asked.

"You and I have the only guns," Scott told his brother. "So you should ride with Sean. I need one person to ride shotgun with me."

"I'll do it," Joe volunteered.

"Okay," Mark said. "That means Luke is with us."

Luke nodded his head.

"I'll go first," Scott said, and handed his shotgun to Joe. "Cover me."

Scott peered beyond the black zombie through the window on the door, and spotted two other walking corpses. One was in the carport beside Scott's car, and the other was staggering slowly up the driveway toward the carport. Scott hesitated for a moment, and then swung the door open with a powerful jerk, knocking the black zombie off of the stairs onto its back. He ran toward his car and slid across the hood toward the driver door.

Joe stepped out of the doorway with the shotgun and blasted a shot through the black zombie's temple, splattering brain matter onto the concrete floor.

Scott opened the driver's door. "Come on!" he shouted. "Let's go!"

Joe ran to the passenger side and opened the door as Scott jumped in and started the engine. Joe remained standing beside the car with his shotgun aimed at the other ghoul in the driveway.

Sean and Luke scrambled to the van as Mark aimed his Glock carefully at the other zombie's head. He fired a single shot, penetrating the creature's forehead, and it collapsed limply to the concrete below.

Sean started the engine as the other two guys jumped in the back of the van. He threw it into reverse and hit the gas just as several zombies came around the corner from the front yard. The van's tires screeched loudly as it backed up quickly into the driveway, filling the air with smoke and the smell of burnt rubber.

Scott followed suit and put his car in reverse, smashing into a zombie on the way out. His tires ran over the ghoul's legs, shattering its shin bones with a loud crunch.

The two vehicles sped down the driveway onto the main road in a cloud of dust. The main road was normally busy with traffic, but there were no other cars in sight now. While driving through the small town, the young men noticed a few ghouls wandering aimlessly on the sides of the road. But as they left the town behind and no more houses or businesses were in sight, there was nothing but trees.

As the two vehicles got closer to the city, Sean slowed down. "We'll to have to get gas soon," he said, turning to Mark and Luke. "I only have a quarter of a tank."

"Let's check out that store up ahead," Mark replied. The Gas Mart was the first gas station on the southern outskirts of the city.

"What's he doing?" Scott wondered out loud as he and Joe watched Sean's van slow down almost to a complete stop in front of the Gas Mart. Scott pulled up beside the van and Joe rolled down his window.

"What's going on?" Joe asked.

Sean rolled down his window. "We need to get gas." He pointed to the gas gauge on his dashboard.

Scott and Joe looked over at the gas station.

"Let's check it out," Scott called out from the driver's seat. "I'm almost out of cigarettes, anyway." He pulled sharply into the gas station parking lot. As they drove into the deserted parking lot, they noticed one of the large glass windows had been busted out.

"Looks like it's been broken into," Scott said matter-of-factly. "But I don't see any of those creatures."

Sean parked his van in front of the gas pumps as Scott and Joe got out of the car.

"I'll turn on the pump for you," Joe shouted across the parking lot, with the shotgun in his hands. He walked up to the broken window and peered into the dark store. The lights were off, but a sufficient amount of sunlight leaked through the tall windows to see reasonably well. He stepped through the broken window, and shards of glass crunched loudly beneath his shoes as he walked.

Most of the shelves inside the store were empty, except for a few opened candy bars and crumpled-up magazines. Trash and other debris littered the floor. Joe spotted the gas pump switch next to an empty cigarette display shelf. He rested the shotgun on the counter next to the cash register, and hopped over the counter. His feet landed on something soft, and he tripped forward face-first, but broke his fall with his forearms.

A cold hand suddenly grabbed him by the ankle. He rolled over quickly onto his back.

An older woman with a pale-colored face crept slowly toward him on the floor. Her hand clenched tightly onto his jeans. She was wearing a red work uniform with a Gas Mart logo on the left side of her chest. Dark, crusty blood stained her left cheek and neck, which originated from a gaping wound in her temple. Her sandy blonde hair was a tangled, frizzy mess. She snarled at Joe in a harsh, raspy tone as she tugged on his pants.

"Shit!" Joe yelled, yanking his foot from the woman's grasp. He backed away frantically from the dead-looking woman, his feet slipping on the smooth tile floor. His back smashed into a wooden shelf, sending rolls of blank receipt paper crashing to the floor.

The hideous woman suddenly lunged at Joe, but her face smashed squarely into the heel of his shoe. He sprung up quickly and jumped to the other side of the counter, grabbing his shotgun in the process. He frantically cocked the pump on the shotgun and aimed it toward the counter, but the woman stayed hidden from sight on the floor behind the counter.

"What's going on in there?" a voice suddenly burst out from the broken window in front of the store.

Startled, Joe turned to see the silhouette of Scott standing in front of the store, who was peering through the open window into the relatively dark store. His eyes squinted as the sun shined brightly above him.

Joe turned back to face the counter, and the deathly-pale woman was standing right in front of him, staring blankly. She reached out to grab him with her long, skinny arms, but he took a step back and aimed the shotgun at her face. He quickly pulled the trigger, blasting a load of buckshot into the woman's skull. Dark crimson blood and small brain fragments splattered onto the counter as the woman's body fell backward, crashing into the cigarette display case.

"You okay in there?" Scott yelled through the window. Sean and Mark joined Scott at the window.

"Yeah," Joe replied, his heart pounding with adrenaline. "I'm fine." He cocked the shotgun, expelling the spent shell as a wisp of smoke rose from the barrel, passing through a beam of sunlight. "Looks like looters sacked this place. They took just about everything, including the cigarettes."

"Damn it!" Scott cursed.

"Wait a minute," Joe said, reaching across the counter. "Here's something for you." He tossed a half-empty box of butane lighters to Scott.

"Thanks," Scott said with a smirk. He retrieved a cigarette from his shirt pocket and lit it.

"What happened?" Sean asked, sounding concerned. "We heard a gunshot."

"It was just another one of those creatures," Joe answered. "I took care of it."

"We'd better get a move on it," Mark advised. "There might be more of 'em."

"Hang on," Joe said. "I'll turn on the pumps." He set the shotgun back down and hopped over the counter. Stepping over the dead woman's body, he hit the pump switch, and jumped back across the counter.

As the four young men walked back to their vehicles, Luke emerged from the bushes outside the store.

"I had to take a leak," Luke said as he zipped his fly. "Is everything all right?"

"Everything's fine," Mark replied. "Let's get back in the van."

Joe got back in Scott's car, and Luke and Mark loaded up in Sean's van. After Sean and Scott finished filling up with gas, they drove off back onto the main road toward the city. Scott took the lead again, and Sean followed closely behind.

As they drove deeper into the city, they began to see more undead creatures wondering about aimlessly on the sidewalks and in the parking lots of shopping centers and grocery stores. Old newspapers and other trash littered the streets and empty lots, blowing around in the gentle breeze. The unmistakable smell of death permeated the mid-morning air.

"Roll up the windows," Sean sputtered, wrinkling his face in disgust. Mark and Luke complied as they held their noses.

In the car ahead, Scott picked up speed as the numbers of the walking dead increased. They were driving into a more densely populated area of the city, and some of the zombies were starting to mill around in the streets. Scott's car plowed into several of the mindless ghouls, hurling their mangled bodies into the air. The car smashed into a fat, shirtless zombie with a loud thud. Its big head made a small crack in the windshield.

"Careful," Joe said, "we don't want to wreck."

"Don't worry," Scott insisted. "I know what I'm doing."

As they continued on, they noticed more and more carnage and destruction. Wrecked cars lined both sides of the street. Some of them were smashed up, some were overturned, and some of them were even on fire or were still smoking. The windows of many of the stores and other buildings had been smashed out, covering the sidewalks with shards of glass. Hordes of the undead walked the streets, some of them chewing on pieces of severed human limbs. Pools of blood and gore littered the sidewalks in various places.

"Jesus," Luke said with a sigh. "This is a fucking nightmare."

"I hope we make it to the rescue station alive," Mark remarked, shaking his head.

"It's not much farther," Sean pointed out. In the distance, random bursts of gunfire could be heard.

"Well that's comforting," Luke said with a hint of sarcasm in his voice.

As the two vehicles turned onto Tennessee Street, Leon High School came into view. Outside the large school, a group of men dressed in camouflage fatigues stood lined up behind a chain link fence, firing short bursts from their automatic rifles at the zombies outside. A number of corpses lay rotting on the street.

Joe breathed a sigh of relief. "At least the National Guard is doing their job."

As the vehicles approached the front gate to the school, a soldier raised his rifle and waved at them with his other hand. Scott rolled down his window and stuck his head out of the car. One of the soldiers picked off a zombie that was approaching the car.

"We'll open the gate for you in a minute," the soldier told Scott. "In the meantime, just sit tight." The soldier walked over to what appeared to be his commanding officer. A couple of ghouls approached the idle vehicles, but were immediately taken down by a burst of gunfire.

From the van behind Scott, Sean leaned his head out the window and shrugged at Scott, as if to ask, "What's the deal?"

Scott waved at him and turned to Joe. "Put the shotgun under the seat," he ordered.

"I don't think they care…" Joe muttered.

"Just do it."

Joe complied.

Another zombie walked toward Scott's car with its arms outstretched like Frankenstein, but a bullet ripped through its skull before it could even touch the car. One of the soldiers put his hand to his ear as he received a message though his earpiece. He waved at another soldier, signaling him to unlock the gate. Two other soldiers walked to the gate. Once it was unlocked, they paused for a moment as the other soldier motioned at Scott to move forward. They slid the gate open as other soldiers fired shots at approaching zombies.

"Let's haul ass!" Scott yelled, stepping on the gas pedal. The two vehicles sped through the gate and the soldiers quickly closed it behind them. One of the soldiers locked the gate while the others fired their weapons at the approaching ghouls. Another soldier held up his hand, motioning for Scott to stop his car.

Scott put the car in neutral and rolled down his window. "Where should we park?"

"Please step out of the vehicle," the soldier replied.

"Okay…" Scott hesitated for a moment, and then turned the car off. He started to take the keys out of the ignition.

"Leave the keys in the vehicle," the soldier ordered.

Scott took his hands off the keys and sighed. "You want me to get out?"

"Yes," the soldier replied. "Both of you step out…we'll take it from here."

Scott opened the door and got out while Joe glanced under the seat to make sure the shotgun was still hidden.

"Come on," the soldier grunted. "Let's go." Joe stepped out of the car and joined Scott. Another soldier got in the driver's seat and drove off through the school parking lot.

"What is this shit?" Mark ranted inside the van.

Sean shrugged. A soldier walked up to the driver's window of the van and motioned for Sean to get out. Sean opened his door.

"Where are you taking our cars?" Mark inquired from the passenger's seat.

"Just step out of the vehicle, sir," the soldier advised. Two more soldiers stepped up on each side of the van. One of them opened the sliding door. Luke stepped out and one of the soldiers took him by the arm and guided him over to where Scott and Joe stood.

"This is bullshit," Mark sputtered as the other soldier opened the passenger's door and reached for Mark's arm. Mark pushed him away and walked over to join his friends. The soldier gave him a dirty look and shut the passenger's door.

Sean left the engine running and joined his companions while one of the soldiers got in the van and drove off.

"They're just doing their job," Luke whispered.

"Fuck their job," Mark snapped.

"Do you have identification?" the soldier inquired.

"You mean like a driver's license?" Scott asked.

"Yes."

"Here," Scott said, handing him his license. The other young men gave them their licenses as well. One of the soldiers took the identification cards and wrote something down on a clipboard.

"This way," another soldier dictated as he held his rifle in one hand, motioning with his other hand for the young men to follow him. They walked to the front entrance of the school, where two armed guards stood on each side of the doors. They opened the doors as the men approached. As the doors opened, the loud roar of a crowd could be heard from inside.

"Go on in," the escorting soldier urged, standing still when he reached the doors. The young men walked inside the lobby, except for Mark, who was pushed in by one of the guards. Inside, another guard stood at the entrance with an M-16 strapped to his shoulder.

The young men stood at the entrance and looked around. The building was crowded and noisy. Children ran around inside yelling and playing, while their parents tried to keep up with them. Some of the people were arguing loudly, while others tried to intercede. A few elderly people sat quietly in the corners, looking as if they wanted to die.

Mark spotted a female rescue worker walking nearby. "Excuse me, ma'am," he addressed the worker, grabbing her by the arm. "Where can I find out if my family is here?"

The woman paused, pulling her arm from the big man's grasp.

"The administration desk is in the main lecture hall," she said, pointing down a hallway in the back of the lobby.

"Thanks," Mark said over his shoulder.

The five friends made their way back to the hallway, pushing through the crowd of sweaty, unkempt people. The hall was lined with glass cases filled with trophies that the high school sports team had won. Black and white pictures adorned the walls, proudly displaying team pictures from previous school years. Several people were trying to sleep on blankets which had been laid out on the floor between the trophy cases as loud voices echoed down the hallway from the lecture hall. The hallway reeked of body odor and old food.

"I don't like this place," Luke grumbled, holding his nose.

As the men walked into the lecture hall, they saw even more disorder and confusion. People were yelling and screaming at one another. Several guards with automatic rifles dangling from their shoulders were escorting people out of the room by force, while others restrained a couple of unruly civilians.

A shorter man collided face-first into Mark's chest as he was attempting to run out of the room. He stumbled backward for a moment and then tried to keep running, but was immediately tackled by a uniformed guard.

"Follow me," Mark instructed, pointing to a desk in the rear. A heavyset woman with light-brown hair and a cigarette dangling from her mouth sat at the messy desk, which was covered in file folders and loose pieces of paper. Mark walked up to the desk and leaned against it, examining the fat, busy woman. The woman didn't even notice the five men standing in front of her and continued writing. Mark cleared his throat loudly.

The large woman pushed her thick reading glasses up with one finger and looked up at the men standing at the desk. "Can I help you, gentlemen?" She had a thick southern accent.

"I'm looking for my family," Mark answered. "Can you tell me if they are here?"

"Just a moment," the big woman replied. Without standing up, she rolled her desk chair over a few feet to another desk and typed something into a computer. She glanced back up at Mark. "What are their names?"

"Douglass and Sally Walker," Mark responded.

The woman entered the names into the computer and scrolled down the screen for a few moments. She took a deep drag from her cigarette and rested it in an ashtray on the desk.

"Here we go," the woman said, pointing at the blue screen. "They were here a few days ago, but it looks like they were transported to an undisclosed location."

"*Undisclosed* location?" Scott asked, raising his eyebrows. "What the hell is that?"

"We have busses running everyday," the woman replied. "We don't keep records of where all the civilians go."

"Where are they taking them?" Mark inquired, stepping up to the desk.

"They could be anywhere," the woman replied. "When the building fills up, we have to move people to other stations."

"Look here," Mark said, pounding his fist on the woman's desk. "Just tell me how I can find my family."

"I'm sorry sir," the big woman replied, shrugging her shoulders. "You can wait for the next bus and look for them at another shelter. Other than that, I just don't know how to help you."

"You can give us our cars so we can get the hell out of this shithole," Scott snapped, stepping toward the fat woman.

An armed guard grabbed Scott by the arm, holding him back.

"I'm sorry," the woman said sincerely. "But you're not allowed to leave. There's a martial law in effect."

Mark punched the wall with his fist, and the guard gave him a threatening look. The big man stepped back, staring vacantly out of a window. After a moment of silence, he turned to walk away.

"Hold on," the big woman said, putting out her cigarette. "You might want to try the church."

Mark stopped walking and faced the woman again.

"Huh?" he asked.

"The First Baptist Church," the woman said. "The last bus went there—on College Avenue."

"How can we get there?"

"I told you, you can get on the next bus. It may stop at the church, but I'm not positive."

"When does the next bus leave?"

"Two weeks."

"Two *weeks*?" Mark rolled his eyes and sighed deeply.

Luke, Joe, and Sean gave the woman the names of their family members, but none of them showed up in her records. Discouraged, the men walked back out of the lecture hall into an adjacent room and exited through a door leading to a courtyard.

Outside, a group of young black men were playing basketball on a concrete court. The area was enclosed by a chain link fence with barbed wired coils along the top. A group of National Guard troops were standing beside a large fire on the other side of the fence.

"We should have gotten here sooner," Mark said, looking down at the grass.

Scott lit a cigarette, exhaling smoke into the wind.

"At least we survived," Sean said, placing his hand on Mark's shoulder.

"Yeah," Joe agreed. "We could have ended up like one of *them*." He pointed at the huge fire beyond the fence.

The troops were carrying dead bodies from the bed of a large pickup truck and casting them into the flames.

"Jesus Christ," Luke gasped. "The world has gone to shit."

"We've got to get out of this place," Scott said, puffing on his cigarette.

"How are we gonna do that?" Joe asked.

"I don't know," Scott replied. "But I'm sure as hell not staying here."

**Nathan Tucker**

# 6

"They're serving dinner in the cafeteria," Mark said.

"I know," Scott replied. "Hang on." He took a deep drag of his cigarette, keeping his gaze fixed intently on the guards as they patrolled the fence at the end of the courtyard. One of the guards opened the gate as another guard left, changing shifts. Scott glanced at his watch, making a special note of the time at which the shift-change had occurred.

"Come on, man!" Mark said. "We're gonna miss it if we don't hurry."

"Yeah, I'm coming." Scott flicked his cigarette butt onto the ground and followed his brother inside. Sean, Joe, and Luke were already in line in the cafeteria when the Walker brothers entered.

The young men had only been staying at the rescue station for two days, but they had noticed most of the people becoming increasingly irritable and restless. A couple of small fights had broken out the previous night, but they were quickly broken up by guards. Those involved in the fight were taken away by the guards, and it was still unclear to the young men where they were keeping them. Scott was especially curious as to the detained men's whereabouts, but he had kept silent about it. As he entered the cafeteria, he kept a suspicious eye trained on the two guards at the entrance.

The large mess hall buzzed loudly with the roar of voices. The room was filled with people, and some of them were eating on the floor against the walls because all of the tables were taken. Most of the people looked disheveled and unkempt, as if they had been on the run for days before they had come to the station. There was a long line of people along the wall waiting to get food from the kitchen.

Some of the people were arguing with one another at the tables. Their loud voices could be heard clearly above the roar of the crowd. Even some young children were bickering, pushing and grabbing one another as they fought over a small piece of candy.

A family with two small children finished eating and got up from one of the tables. A scruffy-looking older man rushed to the table to sit down in the open place, but he bumped into a younger man wearing a white wife-beater shirt, causing him to drop his tray of food.

"Hey," the young man said, pushing the older man. "Watch it, buddy!"

"Get out of my way," the older man said, and pushed the man back. The younger man fell back into someone else's tray, spilling food and water all over the table.

The young man jumped back up and punched the older man in the face, knocking him back into a woman who was eating nearby. The woman's husband stood up and punched the older man, and soon a large fight broke out in the cafeteria.

"Jesus Christ!" Mark said, watching as the fight quickly escalated into an all-out brawl. Food flew across the room, and random strangers were jumping in on the action.

"Let's go," Scott said, and the young men left the scene of chaos, heading for the rear exit. Just as they reached the door, two soldiers burst through into the cafeteria, wielding billy-clubs.

"Shit!" Luke said, stopping dead in his tracks. One of the soldiers raised his club to strike Luke, but Mark's fist caught him square in the jaw. The soldier staggered back a few steps, and the five young men dashed through the door into the courtyard. Just as the door closed, mob of angry brawlers descended upon the two soldiers, and fists and clubs flew in every direction. The cafeteria filled with the rowdy sound of fighting.

"This place is insane," Scott said as the young men walked out into the courtyard. He lit a cigarette as a small group of soldiers wearing riot gear and wielding clubs rushed past them toward the cafeteria.

"Maybe so," Luke agreed. "But not as crazy as it is out there." He pointed to the large fence at the edge of the courtyard, where a large group of zombies stood clawing and biting at the metal chain links.

"Are you sure?" Mark asked. He peered through the barred windows of the cafeteria, where the guards in riot gear were hitting people, including elderly men and women, with their clubs. The other four young men joined Mark at the windows and gazed inside.

"Jesus," Joe exclaimed as he watched the soldiers corral groups of people into corners, and lead them into the nearby locker rooms where they imprisoned them.

"I guess they've turned the locker rooms into makeshift holding cells," Sean said.

"Yeah," Scott affirmed. "We'd better be careful. I don't want to end up a prisoner in this shit hole."

"We're prisoners anywhere we go," Luke said, raising his voice for emphasis. "At least we're protected here."

Another small band of soldiers rushed past the young men, brushing against them as they moved into the cafeteria to reinforce their comrades. These soldiers wore gas masks, and one of the men was strapped with canisters of tear gas.

"Watch it!" Scott protested, and he pushed one of the soldiers that had bumped into him. The soldier spun around quickly, drawing a nightstick from his belt. He stared Scott down from behind his dark gas mask as he patted the baton in his hand menacingly.

Mark and Sean stepped up beside Scott with clenched fists, and the soldier backed away slowly. Finally, after a few uneasy moments of staring, the soldier turned and ran into the cafeteria to join his companions.

"That's right," Scott yelled through the door. "Keep running!" Sean and Mark both looked at Scott and rolled their eyes.

Luke breathed a sigh of relief as the door to the cafeteria closed, and the rowdy noise of yelling and fighting from inside became a muffled buzz. "Be careful," he said as he turned to face Scott.

"Don't worry," Scott replied, cutting him off. "Everything's under control." He took one last puff of his cigarette and flicked the butt into the bushes. He walked along the edge of the brick building until he came upon an array of small windows, high above the bushes lining the wall. "Give me a boost," he said to his brother.

Mark hesitated for a moment, glancing around the courtyard. There were no guards in sight. He walked over to his brother and cupped his hands for him. Scott stepped up on Mark's hands and peered through a high window. At first, all he could see was the tops of some metal lockers. But as he pulled himself up higher for a closer look, he caught sight of a group of people crowded around a closed doorway. Some of the people were banging on the door, which appeared to be locked. It appeared as though many of the people had given up trying to escape the confines of the locker room, and were lying down on benches. The ones that couldn't find a bench to lie on simply lay on the cold tile floor. But what Scott saw in the corner of the room made his heart skip a beat. He jerked back away from the window in surprise, almost falling from his brother's hands.

"Jesus," Scott gasped.

"What?" Joe asked.

"They've got 'em all locked up in there—every one of 'em."

"What else can they do?" Luke asked. "They've got their hands full as it is."

"It's not right!" Scott cried. He jumped down onto the ground and pushed Luke toward the wall. "Have a look for yourself."

Luke paused for a moment, staring blankly at Scott. Then he shook his head and climbed up onto the window sill with a little help from Mark's strong hands. He cupped his fingers around his eyes and peered through the window across the locker room. When he saw the cages in the corner of the room, couldn't believe his eyes. At first, he thought there were living people in the cages, but after examining them for a moment, he noticed the pale color of their skin, the blood stains on their clothes, and even a few missing limbs on their sickly bodies. He quickly realized that the cages contained members of the living dead.

"Shit!" Luke exclaimed, unable to take his eyes off of the cages. After a few moments, he jumped down, and the other young men climbed up to the windows to get a look for themselves.

"What are they planning to do?" Mark asked.

"I think it's pretty obvious," Scott replied. "But I'm not sticking around to find out for sure!"

"Is the cafeteria clear yet?" Luke asked. "I'm starving."

Scott walked back over to the windows in front of the cafeteria and peered though the glass. He raised his hand and motioned for the others to join him.

"How's it look?" Joe asked as he approached Scott.

"Looks like they've got it under control. We'd better get in there before they stop serving food, though."

The five young men walked into the cafeteria and got in line, which was now very short compared to the first time.

Soon, they got their food trays and sat down together at an empty table.

"This shit tastes like rubber," Scott said through a mouthful of mashed potatoes.

"Better than the T.V. dinners we were eating at your house," Luke said, and Scott gave him an unpleasant look.

"I'd prefer the food at home any day over this," Mark broke in. "But it's better than nothing. At least we *have* food…and a place to sleep."

"Which reminds me," Sean said, "we'd better get to the sleeping area before it fills up."

The young men finished their meals and made their way toward the large gymnasium at the end of the west wing of the school, which had been designated as an area for people to sleep. The gym floor was covered with a vast array of cots, sleeping bags, and various personal belongings of the people who were staying at the rescue station. Although several large fans that were mounted high up on the walls were running loudly, moving air in from outside, the large room was still hot from all the body heat in the room. Besides the constant drone from the fans, other noises filled the gym echoed off the concrete walls and wooden floor. A number of babies were crying as their mothers tried in vain to coax them to stop. Loud voices reverberated about the large room, as families argued with one another, and other people seemed to yell for no apparent reason.

"Well," Mark said as the young men entered into the gym, "looks like we're in for another peaceful night of sleep." He rolled his eyes as he pushed through a small crowd of teenagers that were conversing loudly near the door.

"Hey," one of the teenage boys said as Mark brushed past him. "Watch your step, homey." The boy was dressed in baggy clothes, and wore a backwards cap.

Mark kept walking, ignoring the teenager as his four companions walked around the teenagers and followed him toward an area with several empty cots.

"Yo, homey," the kid said, following behind the five young men with his hands stretched out at his sides as if to pick a fight. "I'm talkin' to you."

Mark turned around, standing up to his full height, and stared down at the teenager. The kid backed up a step or two as the big man stared him down.

"Hey, man," Joe said, walking up beside Mark. "We don't want any trouble, all right?"

"Tell that to your homey," the teenager said as he shoved Mark with one of his hands. As soon as he had pushed the big man, he found himself on the floor. Mark had pushed him back with such a powerful shove that he fell flat on his back.

"That's enough," Joe said, placing a hand on Mark's shoulder. But the look on the big man's face said otherwise.

"You just fucked up real bad, homeboy," the teenager said as he pulled something from his pocket. He flicked a switch on the object, and a blade popped out. The kid waved the switchblade around, taunting the big, curly-haired man.

Without uttering a word, Mark quickly grabbed the boy's wrist in a powerful grip. In a single motion, he whipped the boy's arm around behind his back, twisting it up at the elbow into a painful contortion. The kid screamed as the big man applied more pressure to his arm, forcing him to drop the knife. Mark snatched up the blade with his other hand without letting go of the boy's arm, and put the knife in his back pocket.

"Try that again," Mark said sternly into the boy's ear, "and next time you won't be so lucky. I'll break your arm in two, if I have to."

"Please," the boy pleaded, "let me go!" His eyes welled up with tears from the sharp pain in his arm.

"Get the fuck outta here, punk," the big man ordered, and he pushed the boy back toward his small group of friends that had been observing from a distance. The boy scampered off, running right past his friends, too embarrassed to face them. As he rushed through the door exiting the gym, his friends chuckled.

Mark walked over to an empty cot alongside his companions and sat down, taking off his shirt. "Punk-ass kids."

"I don't like this place," Sean said as he lay down on a cot. "We'd better watch our backs all the time."

"We won't have to pretty soon," Scott said matter-of-factly.

"What's he talking about?" Luke asked.

Sean shrugged and shook his head. The others were already lying in their cots, trying to go to sleep.

"Just trust me," Scott said. "It'll all get better real soon."

# 7

After three grueling nights at the rescue station, the five men were growing restless. They seemed to run into trouble around every corner. Scott, especially, was becoming increasingly irritable. He couldn't stand the way the soldiers herded people around like sheep. To add to his disdain for them, he could only imagine what they had done to the people in the locker room. Each day, he kept a watchful eye on the guards, paying special attention to the time intervals in which they opened the gates in the courtyard. Through the fence, he could see Sean's gold-colored van in the rear parking lot. He thought he could see his small car beside the van, but he couldn't be sure from the distance in which he stood.

"They're gonna open that gate in exactly ten minutes," Scott whispered, looking at his watch. He glanced up at the metal gate where a soldier stood guard with a rifle on his shoulder.

The five young men had been sitting on the brick steps outside the cafeteria hall for a few minutes getting some fresh air.

"So?" Luke said sarcastically. He plucked a branch from a nearby bush, fiddling with the leaves out of boredom.

"We're getting out of here today," Scott calmly replied. He pulled a cigarette out of his shirt pocket and cupped his hands around his mouth as he lit it.

Mark's ears perked up at his brother's words. His eyes darted around, studying the guards on the other side of the fence as they went about their daily routine. He was a lot bigger than most of the soldiers, but he knew that they had a lot of combat training.

"You're crazy," Luke said, lowering his voice. "Where the hell would we go?"

"Anywhere away from this place," Scott replied without a second thought. He wiped the sweat from his brow as the hot midday sun shined brightly in the cloudless sky.

Sean and Joe leaned forward slightly as they sat behind the other men, quietly listening to the conversation. They too were growing restless in the confines of the rescue station.

Scott glanced at his watch again, taking a long drag from his cigarette.

"Things may not be perfect here," Luke said, "but at least we're safe. We shouldn't be in any hurry to leave."

"We're *not* safe here," Scott said with a grimace. "We'll end up as food for those things in the cages if we don't watch it."

"And we won't end up as food for them out there?" Luke asked, raising his hands in frustration.

"I don't think I could wait another week for one of those busses," Mark said, shaking his head slowly. "This place is driving me crazy. I wouldn't mind checking out that church, either. It couldn't be any worse than over there. And who knows? Maybe our families are there. Whatever happens, we need to get the hell out of this place. They can't keep us here like this. It just ain't right."

Scott stood up, pacing the sidewalk in front of the steps. He puffed anxiously on his cigarette, eyeing his watch every so often.

"No way, man," Luke said, fixing his eyes firmly on an M-16 carried by one of the troops that was marching along the chain link fence. "There's no chance in hell of us getting past those guards."

Scott finished his cigarette and tossed in on the grass. He glanced at his watch and walked toward the gate.

"Where are you going?" Luke called out, but Scott ignored him.

The trooper that had been marching alongside the fence stopped when he reached the metal gate. He unhooked a keychain from his belt and unlocked the gate as another guard pushed it open from inside the courtyard.

"Excuse me," Scott said, walking up to the guards as the gate swung open. "You got a cigarette?"

The soldiers looked over at him, pausing at the gate. One of the men slung his rifle over his shoulder, reaching into his jacket pocket.

"Thanks buddy," Scott said, walking up next to the guard. He put his hand behind his back, motioning inconspicuously for his friends to join him.

"He's insane," Luke said in a soft voice, rolling his eyes. He and the other young men walked slowly toward the gate.

The guard retrieved a cigarette from his jacket and handed it to Scott.

"Thanks, man," Scott said, putting the cigarette in his mouth. He turned around as if to walk away, and then spun back around. "Sorry, you got a light?"

Both soldiers reached into their camouflage pants, fishing for a lighter, as Scott stepped closer to them.

Suddenly, Scott grabbed one of the guard's wrists, twisting his arm behind his back. The soldier reached for his pistol holster, but Scott quickly slammed his face into the gate, causing him to lose his balance.

"Oh, shit," Luke sighed, his demeanor suddenly changing. He walked slowly toward the gate, adrenaline pumping into his veins.

Mark rushed up to the other guard before he could sling the rifle strap off his shoulder. He punched the solider square in the jaw with a powerful blow, sending the man crashing backward into the fence.

"Get his gun!" Scott yelled, kicking the other guard in the back of the head. The force of the blow knocked the man's face down into the dirt.

Mark snatched the rifle off of the guard's shoulder as Sean and Joe pinned him against the fence.

Luke dropped to his knees, snapping the pistol holster open on the other guard while Scott pinned the man to the ground by stepping on his head. Luke grabbed the Beretta pistol out of the holster and aimed at the soldier's head.

Scott stepped back and the man sat up, raising his hands in submission.

"Hey, man," the guard pleaded. "Just stay cool, all right? Don't do anything stupid."

"On the ground," Luke ordered, "face down!"

The trooper complied without hesitation.

Mark poked the other guard in the chest with the barrel of the M-16, and the man backed up against the fence, raising his hands in the air.

"The keys to the cars..." Scott barked. "Where are they?"

One of the soldiers nodded his head nervously, motioning toward a small wooden shack outside the gate.

Joe rushed over to the little wooden building, disappearing inside. He returned a few seconds later with a large set of keys, and tossed them to Scott.

Suddenly, another guard appeared in the courtyard from the cafeteria door. He fired a warning shot over the heads of the young men.

Mark returned a barrage of fire, and the attacker dove behind a concrete staircase.

Luke grabbed one of the guards, pressing the handgun to the man's temple.

"Drop the gun!" he yelled to the guard in hiding.

There was a moment of silence they waited for a response. Then Luke pointed the handgun into the air and fired two shots. He pressed the pistol back firmly into his hostage's cheek.

Slowly, the soldier behind the staircase raised his hands and tossed the rifle on the ground in front of him.

"Let's go!" Scott ordered, walking quickly toward the fenced-in parking lot.

Sean and Joe sprinted after Scott while Mark and Luke backed away slowly, their guns trained on the guards. The guards stood frozen, their hands raised high in the air.

As Scott approached the lot of vehicles, he leafed through the set of keys and unhooked the key to his car and the key to Sean's van. He tossed the rest of the keys on the ground and dashed toward the vehicles.

Scott and Joe jumped in the car, and Scott tossed the other key to Sean. The men started their cars and revved up the engines as Mark and Luke stopped halfway, keeping their guns aimed at the guards. A few seconds later, the van pulled up, and Mark and Luke jumped inside.

As soon as the men were inside the vehicles, the guards rushed back toward the cafeteria. Several bullets from Mark's rifle whizzed over their heads, and they dropped back to the ground.

"The gate is locked," Scott said as he rounded the corner, swerving to avoid a guard, who dove out of the way.

Joe reached under the seat and found the shotgun right where he had left it. As Scott slammed on the brakes in front of the main gate, Joe leaned out the window and took aim at the lock.

Suddenly, a bullet crashed through the windshield, narrowly missing Joe's torso. Joe turned to the side quickly, aiming his shotgun at the source of gunfire.

A guard peeked around the corner of a nearby building, firing another burst of shots from his handgun, but Joe ducked.

Two bullets suddenly ripped through the guard's thigh, and Joe turned around to see Mark, who was standing up through the sunroof of the van with his M-16. The guard dropped his weapon, falling to the ground in agony.

"Let's go!" Mark cried, pointing forward.

Joe turned back around and shot the lock off the gate with a single blast from the shotgun. Scott stepped on the gas, and the car took off onto the main road, the van following closely behind. The vehicles plowed through a small crowd of zombies as they sped off.

"Shit!" Luke cried, peering through the rear window of the van. "We've got company!"

Sean glanced in the rearview mirror, noticing an army-green Hummer on their tail several hundred feet behind them. The four-lane highway was empty except for a few abandoned cars along the sides of the road. Sean pressed on the gas and drove up alongside Scott, pointing at the vehicle behind them.

"Follow me," Scott insisted as he cracked his window. He made a sharp turn into a neighborhood, and Sean followed, his tires squealing as the van slid into the turn.

"Look out!" Mark cried from the back seat, but it was too late to stop. The van crashed into a mailbox, forming a crack down the middle of the windshield. But the van kept speeding forward.

Mark and Luke stood up through the sunroof, watching as the Hummer turned the corner in hot pursuit. Mark fired several wild shots from his rifle, but the bullets just whizzed by the speeding vehicle, ricocheting off the concrete into the air.

Suddenly, Scott drove off the road into a concrete drainage canal, and Sean followed suit. As the pursuing vehicle approached, Luke aimed carefully the windshield and fired again and again until the gun was out of ammo. He squeezed the trigger several times, but the gun just clicked, so he tossed it at the Hummer. The gun bounced off the vehicle's windshield, making a small crack in the glass.

A soldier in the passenger's seat of the Hummer leaned out of the window, letting loose a barrage of gunfire as the two young men ducked back into the van. The rear window of the van shattered, and the bullets imbedded into the backseat.

Mark stood up again through the sunroof, taking aim at the vehicle behind him. He flicked a switch on the rife, setting it to three-round burst. He fired several burst-shots, and this time, the bullets smashed through the windshield of the Hummer, missing its occupants by a thin margin. He fired once more, aiming at the driver's side, and the bullets crashed through the glass again. The windshield turned red with blood and the Hummer swerved to the side, crashing head-on into a concrete overpass.

Scott slowed down, gazing into his rearview mirror. When he was saw that their pursuers were out of commission, he drove back onto the neighborhood road. He came to a stop in an area where no creatures were in sight, and the gold van pulled up beside him. They sat idle for a few moments, catching their breath after the adrenaline-rush.

"You guys all right?" Scott asked, rolling his window all the way down.

Sean looked back at his passengers and nodded.

Several zombies began to emerge from the driveways of the surrounding houses.

"We'd better get a move on it," Joe suggested, cocking the shotgun. He fired at one of the creatures as it approached the vehicles, and it staggered backward as the buckshot tore into its abdomen. Several more zombies walked out into the street in front of them.

"All right," Scott agreed, glancing over at Sean. "Let's go." He slammed on the gas pedal, swerving around the walking corpses as he drove. The gold van followed closely behind.

The two vehicles sped through the maze of interconnecting streets in the neighborhood, weaving through abandoned vehicles and wandering zombies. As they drove out onto a main road, the men noticed that the stoplights were out at most of the intersections.

"Looks like the power's off in this area," Sean said, steering clear of an abandoned car.

Scott drove deeper into the city, leading the vehicles toward the downtown area. Turning onto College Avenue, he caught sight of the large church building at the corner of the intersection. A tall palm tree swayed in the wind in front of the building. The church was enclosed by a rugged wooden fence, which looked like it had been recently constructed. As Scott approached the entrance, he realized that the gate was open. He stopped the car at the edge of the sidewalk and the van pulled up beside him.

"Christ," Scott said, shaking his head. He watched as a small army of zombies moved through the churchyard, some of them passing in and out through open double-doors. Some of the creatures carried severed body parts in their hands, gnawing on the bloody human remains as they moved about. Scott looked away in disgust as Joe rolled down the passenger side window.

"If this was the other rescue station," Scott said to Sean, who was hanging out of the driver's seat of the van, "then it's been overrun. We'll have to move on."

Sean nodded and the two vehicles pulled back out onto the road.

"Where the hell are we going?" Luke asked from the backseat as he pushed his glasses up on his face.

"Wherever Scott leads us," Sean replied, sighing.

"We need to go back to the sticks," Mark advised. "There's too many of those things in the city."

The desolate streets were empty except for a few wandering ghouls and abandoned cars. Discarded newspapers and other trash littered the streets and sidewalks, blowing about freely with the wind. The creatures seemed to roam in packs, mainly in the most densely-populated areas of the city. Most of the shops were vacant, their windows broken out. Many of the doors to the buildings hung wide-open as zombies stumbled in and out randomly through the entrances. Even the pawn shops with bars in their windows had been raided.

Joe sat quietly in the passenger's seat as Scott lit another cigarette, picking up speed on the four-lane street. They passed by a large grocery store where all the windows had been broken out. The parking lot was full of ghouls that were wandering about aimlessly. Scott slowed down for a few seconds, but drove off quickly when the creatures started walking toward the car.

"Damned looters," Scott said, exhaling a cloud of smoke as he cracked his window. "They must have hit every store in the city."

"Where are they now?" Joe asked, gazing out through the passenger's window.

Scott sat quietly driving as his mind began to wonder. He imagined all the free merchandise that the looters must have gotten away with—the lucky bastards. If only they had skipped the rescue station. They should have come to the city sooner. There were so many things that they could have used. So many stores they could have hit. But they were too late. The bastards had already cleaned them out.

Another ten minutes passed, but the scenery hadn't changed. The walking dead were everywhere. They lurked around every corner, every intersection, and every alley. Social status placed no bounds upon the numbers of the undead. Hordes of zombies roamed the streets of the rich white neighborhoods, where expensive clothing and jewelry adorned many of their putrid, rotting bodies. Ghouls of all shapes and sizes walked the streets of the poorer neighborhoods as well.

Scott wondered how things had spiraled out of control so quickly. The world around him had come to a sudden halt almost overnight, or so it seemed. It was surreal. To think that a few mindless rotting corpses could shake the very fabric of society, casting civilization into a state of utter chaos within a matter of weeks—it was truly a hellish nightmare.

Scott took a left on the parkway in front of the Florida State Capitol building. Several ghouls dressed in business suits stumbled down the sidewalk as they passed. The once neatly-kept city block was now littered with trash and rubble. Several abandoned cars sat along the sides of the road, still burning as smoke rose from their interior. One of the cars had knocked over a power line, which lay halfway across the road.

The tall Capitol building sat high up on a hill overlooking the city. The four-lane road in front of it stretched down the hill toward the east side of the city. From their vantage point, the young men could see across several blocks, where clouds of smoke rose from random fires spread out among the various apartment complexes and business strips. Wandering ghouls roamed the streets in packs, but the highway ahead was clear enough to pass through.

Gaining momentum as his car careened down the sloping road, Scott weaved between walking corpses, narrowly avoiding their gruesome bodies. The gold van followed closely behind, mimicking the movements of the car in front. As the vehicles sped down the highway, they crossed into the opposite lane to avoid an overturned semi.

"Are we gonna head for the sticks?" Joe asked, breaking the silence in the little car.

"I guess so," Scott replied, sighing. For a fleeting moment, he thought about turning around and heading back the Capitol to see what was left of the place, but he shook the thought from his mind. *Too risky*, he thought. There were bound to be more deserted buildings on the other side of town. Maybe some of the shops hadn't been hit yet. A liquor store would be nice. Or better yet, a gun shop. Guns had become quite a valuable commodity in these terrible times. One might think that food and water would be of foremost concern to a survivalist, but guns and ammunition were at the top of Scott's list. His eyes narrowed as he fantasized about the plunder he hoped to find. He pressed on the gas, picking up speed as the gold van struggled to keep the pace with the smaller car.

"If we're gonna keep moving," Mark said, glancing over Sean's shoulder at the gas gauge, "we'll have to find more fuel."

"We've still got a half-tank," Sean said.

"But if we head out to the country, we'll need it."

"Let's just hope we make it that far."

It was suddenly apparent to Mark that they had no food or water. He wondered what Scott had in mind, but he knew his brother too well to think that he would lead them off to their deaths.

**Nathan Tucker**

The two vehicles sped down the road at nearly eighty miles-per-hour through the outskirts of town as the sun began to set. The clouds in the sky appeared deep red as the sun crept into the horizon. The men in the vehicles were able to see a few zombies in the streets, but their numbers decreased the further they drove from the inner city. There were more trees and wooded areas on the outskirts of town, but there were still quite a few shopping centers and gas stations spread out along the sides of the road.

Sean suddenly slammed on his brakes as Scott's car whipped sharply into a parking lot on the right side of the road.

"What the hell?" Mark exclaimed. He braced himself against the dashboard as the van jolted to a stop.

"What is he thinking?" Sean asked, looking up at the large sign in front of them, which read, "Wal-Mart Supercenter." Underneath the large sign was a smaller sign that read, "Open 24 Hours." Sean pulled into the parking lot, following Scott's car, which was already several hundred feet ahead of them.

"Forget it, man," Mark yelled as he spotted a large crowd of zombies lumbering around in the immense parking lot. "There's too many of those creatures!"

"What's Scott doing?" Luke asked as he leaned forward in the back seat. Scott's car sped right through the crowd of ghouls, smashing violently into several of them, sending their stiff bodies flying across the parking lot. His car broke quickly through the crowd of ghouls and came to a screeching stop directly in front of the gate to the Garden Center. A moment later, Sean drove up beside him. Luke stood up and poked his head out through the sun-roof.

"What the hell are you doing?" Luke demanded as Scott rolled down his window. Joe fired off a shotgun blast through the passenger window at a nearby zombie. The creature dropped limply to the pavement, a pool of blood forming around its head.

"Follow me," Scott said calmly as he motioned for Sean to wait behind him. He revved up his engine several times before letting go of the clutch. The car's tires squealed as smoke rose from the burning rubber. A moment later, the car crashed through the gate, breaking the chain which had held it locked in place. He slammed on the brakes just before the car reached the two glass doors of the store entrance.

"Come on!" Scott yelled as he and Joe jumped out of the car and motioned to Sean to drive in closer. He grabbed a small shovel from a nearby gardening tools display to use as a makeshift melee weapon. Sean parked the van behind Scott's car, and he and the other two passengers jumped out.

"You're crazy, man!" Luke exclaimed, pointing at the mob of zombies that were sluggishly approaching.

"Close the gate!" Scott yelled. "Come on, help me!" He pushed one side of the gate as Mark closed the other side. Joe picked up the broken chain that was lying on the ground and tried to put it back on the gate.

"That's not gonna work," Scott said. The broken chain wasn't long enough to reach around the bars of the gate.

Mark slung the assault rifle off his shoulder and fired a three-round burst into the herd of walking corpses. One of the creatures fell as the bullets plowed through its skull. He pulled the trigger again, but the gun only made a clicking noise. Realizing the magazine cartridge was empty, he slung the rifle strap over his shoulder and drew his pistol.

"You guys watch the gate," Sean suggested, running off down an aisle which was filled with gardening tools. "Don't let them get in!" His voice trailed off as he disappeared behind the aisles.

Luke reluctantly joined the other three men at the gate. "This will never work! How the hell are we going to get out of here?"

"Just shut up and hold the gate," Scott ordered as the crowd of ghouls came menacingly close to the fence. A moment later, several of them had already reached the gate and were reaching through the bars at the young men. Their cold, pale arms flailed around wildly, trying to grab onto some fresh meat.

"Hurry up with that!" Mark yelled out to Sean, who was still nowhere to be seen. One of the cold, disgusting hands grabbed Mark's face, but he slapped it away. He stuck his pistol between the bars of the gate and fired several shots at the creatures.

Suddenly, Sean popped out from behind a shelf. He was carrying a coiled up water hose.

"This should hold up for now," Sean said matter-of-factly as he uncoiled the hose. Scott helped him tie the water hose tightly to the gate while the others held it steady. Once they secured the hose firmly in place, the men stepped back away from the gate and watched the horde of ghouls as they tried in vain to get through the gate.

"Good job," Mark said. "It looks like we're okay for now."

The five men made their way through the Garden Center toward the automatic glass door entrance. As they approached the door, it slid open for them automatically.

"Well, I'll be damned!" Scott exclaimed. "The doors are unlocked."

The men walked cautiously into the large store. It almost seemed like a dream to them as they entered the colorful arena. It was as if they had stepped out of a dark, nightmare world into a brightly lit land of toys and goodies. All of the lights were on inside the store, casting a warm fluorescent glow upon the bountiful supply of goods hoarded within its walls. Pleasant, upbeat music played frivolously through the store's ceiling-mounted speakers. Racks of clothing, aisles of beauty care products, jewelry cases, toys, and electronic gadgets were spread out as far as the eye could see. The five young men stood staring wide-eyed at the bounteous treasures which lay before them.

The once bustling superstore of consumerism had somehow managed to evade detection from the city's vicious gangs of looters. Maybe it was because the store was so far out on the outskirts of the urban sprawl that it had simply been overlooked by potential raiders. Or maybe some people had previously attempted to get in, but had died in the process and had joined the army of walking corpses that now surrounded the place. Either way, it didn't matter to Scott Walker. He had finally found what he had been searching for. The place was now his for the taking.

"Let's go shopping!" Scott exclaimed with obvious excitement in his voice. Mark and Joe cheered loudly, giving each other a high-five.

After a few moments of celebration, the three men quieted down as they noticed that Luke and Sean were not quite as thrilled. Sean stood rigid, his eyes darting around nervously, as Scott raised his shotgun and loaded a shell into the chamber. He broke the silence with a cock of his shotgun, and an empty shell bounced and rolled across the tile floor.

"Jesus Christ," Joe blurted out as he spotted a large group of people in the distance. They were the walking dead—clearly identifiable by their all-too-familiar stride. More zombies appeared from the clothing aisles, joining in the advance toward the five men. Some of them pushed empty shopping carts, mimicking a common action of their former lives. A few of them carried various items they had picked up from the store isles.

"Let's get the hell out of here!" Luke gasped, his voice trembling. Several creatures emerged from the nearby aisles, blocking the exit to the Garden Center.

"Wait a minute!" Scott exclaimed with excitement in his voice. He fired a shotgun blast at a nearby zombie, blowing its body backward into a pyramid display of paper towels. The paper rolls scattered across the floor of the store.

Mark turned and faced the creatures that were blocking the exit. He fired again and again, some of his bullets hitting their target, and some bouncing off the concrete walls. One of the zombies dropped as a bullet tore through its forehead. Mark waited for a moment, aiming carefully at another ghoul's head as it approached. He squeezed the trigger, but the gun only clicked. He squeezed again, but the gun wouldn't fire.

"Damn it!" Mark cursed. "I'm out of ammo!"

"Let's leave this place!" Luke yelled.

"No!" Scott cried. "Follow me to the Sporting Goods!"

"You're insane!"

"Trust me," Scott said as he darted off through the store aisles.

The other four hesitated for a moment, frozen in horror as the army of zombies closed in on them. Then Mark tucked the Glock into his pants and took off running behind Scott. The other three men snapped out of their trance and dashed off toward the Sporting Goods without a second thought. They sprinted past two slow-moving creatures that tried to grab them, but the lone ghouls just weren't fast enough for the agile young men.

When they reached the Sporting Goods, it became apparent why Scott was so eager to go there. He was hovering over a glass display case, wide-eyed with anticipation as he surveyed its contents. The other four men looked around at the wide selection of goods on display. Two large display cases caught their attention—one contained a rack of rifles, and in the other one there was a rack of shotguns. The wooden racks were encased in glass.

"Over here, Mark!" Scott cried. He was standing behind a glass checkout counter with was stocked full of ammunition boxes. As his brother walked up behind him, he pointed through the glass at a stack of boxes with the words "Winchester 9 mm" printed on them.

"Great!" Mark exclaimed. "But how the hell are we gonna get them out of there?"

Scott looked up at his brother and grinned. He lifted the butt of his shotgun and smashed it through the top of the glass counter in a single swift motion.

Mark rolled his eyes and popped the magazine out of his handgun. He dumped a box of bullets out onto the counter and loaded his clip while Scott opened up a box of shotgun shells from a display stack.

"This is no good," Joe said. He was standing beside the rifle display, staring at the arsenal of weapons. "They all have locks on them."

"Then we'll need the keys," Scott answered as he loaded some shells into his shotgun. He filled his pockets with as many shells as he could fit in them.

"Where's Luke?" Sean asked, realizing that Luke was nowhere in sight.

Suddenly, the two ghouls that they had passed by on their way to the Sporting Goods section walked around the corner of an aisle. Scott and Mark let loose a barrage of gunfire, and the two creatures dropped like rag dolls. The four men stood poised as they stared at the lifeless corpses, waiting for more zombies to emerge from the aisles.

A loud crash of shattering glass thundered from behind them. The men spun around and saw Luke holding a hatchet. He had smashed the glass on the rifle display case.

"Where'd you get the axe?" Joe asked his cousin.

"From the hardware department," Luke replied as he walked over to the shotgun display. He swung the hatchet as hard as he could and smashed through the glass containing the rack of shotguns. The shattered glass rained down on the linoleum floor, crackling beneath Luke's shoes as he stepped back. He grabbed a double-barrel shotgun from a rack labeled "Rossi Squire 20-Guage," and emptied a box of 20-guage shotgun shells into his pocket.

"Let's take what we can and get the hell out of here," Joe suggested as he walked over to the rack of rifles. He spun the circular display around, until he spotted a weapon that caught his eye. The rifle had a short barrel and a mounted scope, and the label above it read, "Steyr Arms Scout."

Sean walked up beside Joe and surveyed the arsenal of rifles. A lever-action rifle with a mounted scope caught his attention. The label above the gun read, "Marlin 336A." Sean picked up the gun and walked over to the ammunition counter. He picked out a case of .30-30 rounds for his rifle and tossed a box of .308 Winchester to Joe.

"We need to find the keys to those locks if you guys are going to be able to use the guns," Scott advised. All of the rifles and shotguns had safety locks attached to their firing mechanisms.

"Let's do it," Mark said as he cocked his handgun enthusiastically. He scooped up the rest of the nine-millimeter bullets on the counter and dumped them into his pockets.

Sean and Joe strapped their rifles to their backs. They each grabbed a baseball bat from a nearby aisle, and Luke held onto his hatchet.

"I'm pretty sure the main offices are in the rear of the store," Scott said. "The keys should be back there somewhere." He pointed to a set of double-doors that led to the stockroom.

The five young men looked around cautiously before moving. There were several zombies walking toward them in the distance, but they were so far away that they didn't pose any immediate threat. The men could hear footsteps from behind several aisles, and a several unseen zombies let out ghoulish moans.

Scott fidgeted with his shotgun for a moment, ejecting a jammed shell from the chamber, while the other four waited patiently for his signal to run.

Mark noticed a stack of ammo labeled ".223 Remington." He grabbed a box, remembering that the M-16 was out of bullets. He stuffed the box of ammo in his pocket and glanced over at his brother.

Scott lifted his shotgun in one hand and motioned for the others to go. In unison, the group of young men made a dash for the double-doors, Scott taking the lead.

As they rounded the corner of an aisle, Scott bumped into a wandering creature. The ghoul stumbled backward, and Scott smashed the butt of his gun into the creature's skull, knocking it to the floor. When the group reached the stockroom doors, they stopped running.

Scott and Mark walked up, facing the doors, while the others stepped back, their melee weapons braced for action. Scott and Mark held their guns up high and looked over at each other. Scott nodded at his brother, and Mark kicked the doors open. The two brothers charged through the doors, aiming their weapons this way and that, like a SWAT team making a raid.

The stockroom was dark, and all the brothers could see were boxes and a few empty pallets. It was quiet, and as far as they could see, there were no creatures in sight. The brothers crept cautiously through the maze of boxes as their eyes gradually adjusted to the darkness. The other three men followed closely behind with their weapons in hand.

"It looks clear," Mark said as he flipped a light switch on the wall. The room flickered with dull fluorescent light for a few seconds, creating an eerie scene. Then the room went dark again for a moment and the overhead lamps bathed the stockroom in bright light.

Luke picked up a heavy box from a dark corner of the room and moved it into the light. A label on the box read, "Campbell's Soup."

"At least we won't starve to death," Joe said with a sigh.

"Oh, we're going to eat well," Scott added. "Don't you worry about that." He looked around at all the boxes, wide-eyed like a kid in a candy store.

"How are we going to get this stuff out of here?" Sean asked. "We can't just walk out of here with this stuff."

"You're right," Scott agreed. "That's why we have to stay here."

"What?" Mark cut in. "Are you crazy?"

"There's no way!" Luke cried.

Sean and Joe glanced at each other, shaking their heads.

"Look," Scott said. "We don't have a lot of options here. Those creatures are everywhere. We're gonna have to deal with them anywhere we go."

"That's true," Mark agreed. "But this place is full of them! We stay here and we're just begging for trouble!"

"No," Scott said calmly. "Look around. We have everything we could ever need here. And those creatures are so slow! We can hold them off easily."

"He's right," Sean chimed in. "We held up fine back at the house. The only reason we had to leave is because we ran out of food."

"But this place is so huge!" Joe said, shaking his hands in the air.

"We might be able to stand our ground against those creatures," Luke said. "But what about other people? We're not the only ones who need food and supplies."

Scott opened his mouth to speak but Joe cut him off.

"That's right! Even if we take care of those monsters, there are bound to be looters. And most of them are probably armed!"

"We'll just have to deal with that when the time comes," Scott said, raising his voice. He set his shotgun down on a stack of boxes and picked up one of the large boxes. He walked over to the double doors and placed the box in front of them. He stacked another box on top of it.

Mark tucked his pistol into his jeans and moved to help his brother. He picked up a heavy box containing a large television and stacked it on top of the other boxes.

"Oh, I see," Luke said sarcastically. "We're just going to barricade ourselves in here."

"Yes," Scott replied coldly as he lifted another box. "For now. We haven't eaten all day, and I'm sure a little sleep wouldn't hurt us either."

Sean joined the two brothers and started stacking boxes against the doors.

"This is exactly what we're trying to get away from!" Luke exclaimed, crossing his arms. "We're creating a prison for ourselves!"

Joe dropped his baseball bat and picked up a box. He joined the others as they created a wall of heavy cartons.

"I can't believe we're doing this!" Luke protested. He sighed, standing rigid with his arms crossed tightly. He still held the hatchet in his right hand, watching the others with disapproving eyes as they stacked the last few boxes on the barricade.

As soon as the barricade was complete, the men heard banging noises on the doors. They stepped back and watched as the creatures on the other side of the doors tried in vain to push through. The heavy boxes held up well against the barrage.

Luke's eyes darted back and forth nervously as he held his hatchet tightly in both hands. With each strike against the doors, he tensed up, backing further and further away.

"They can't get through," Sean said as he approached Luke with an outstretched hand. He patted Luke on the shoulder, trying to console him.

"I know," Luke replied, swallowing nervously. "But if enough of them come—they will."

"Don't worry," Scott said from across the room. "This will buy us the time we need. Once we find the keys to the locks on those guns, we'll have enough firepower to really do some damage."

"Great," Luke mumbled in a blatantly sarcastic tone. "I can't wait."

Mark picked up a box cutter from one of the shelves on the wall and opened a nearby box. He dumped the contents onto the concrete floor. The metallic sound of sardines cans hitting the concrete echoed off the thick walls. Mark picked up one of the cans and popped the lid open with its little key. The strong odor of fish filled the room, and the other men scrambled to grab a can for themselves. They were so hungry that they just dumped the contents of the cans into their mouths.

Scott ripped open another container, revealing an assortment of cracker boxes. He eagerly tore into a box of crackers, dumped some sardines on them, and stuffed them into his mouth. The oil from the sardines ran down his chin onto his shirt.

After the men had stuffed their bellies full of food, Mark, Joe and Sean propped themselves up against a stack of boxes and dozed off to sleep.

Scott sat munching on crackers as he stared off into space in deep thought.

"I have to take a leak," Luke said, glancing over at Scott.

Scott nodded silently. His mind was elsewhere.

Luke stood up and scanned the room until he spotted the employee restroom behind a stack of boxes. He approached the room with caution, expecting a zombie to pop out at any moment. He hesitated at the door for a moment, holding his hatchet up in one hand. Slowly, he turned the doorknob, and the door creaked open, revealing the dark restroom. He stepped back and waited, ready for action. But the room was quiet. Cautiously, he reached through the door and felt around blindly on the cold concrete wall until he found the light switch. He flicked it on, and the room lit up, revealing a small, dirty bathroom with a single toilet and a grimy sink. Relieved, he lowered his axe and walked into the room, shutting the door behind him.

After a couple of minutes, Luke returned to the front of the stockroom and found the three men still sleeping against the boxes. But Scott was gone, and his shotgun along with him.

"Scott?" Luke called out, cupping a hand around his mouth. The sound of his voice reverberated around the concrete stockroom. Everything was quiet except for the gentle snoring from Mark's open mouth.

Luke noticed a dim light shining from an open door far across the other side of the stockroom at the end of a dark hallway.

"Scott? Is that you?" Luke's calls received no answer. The room was far enough away that it would have been hard for anyone to hear him from where he was standing. He glanced back at the other men, but they were still fast asleep.

"Damn it," Luke cursed to himself, clenching his teeth. He walked cautiously toward the hallway, stepping over boxes along the way. He entered the dark corridor tentatively, readying his hatchet with both hands.

"Scott?" he called out as his voice echoed down the dimly lit hall. When he reached the open door, he peered around the corner. It was an office, and the only source of light was a small lamp on the desk in the middle of the room. Stacks of papers were scattered all over the desk, and file cabinets lined the wall at the back of the room. Luke walked up to the desk, but Scott was nowhere to be seen.

"Hello?" Luke called out nervously.

Suddenly, a loud crash rang out from the corner of the room behind Luke. He spun around quickly, raising his hatchet high into the air.

"Jesus Christ, man!" Scott gasped, standing in the doorway to a closet next to the door that Luke had entered. "You scared the shit outta me!"

"Sorry," Luke said, panting nervously, his heart pounding with adrenaline.

"Look what I found," Scott said with a smile, holding up a large set of keys.

"The keys to the guns?" Luke asked as his face lightened a little.

"Yep," Scott replied. "And that's not all." He tossed something to Luke. Luke caught the item, dropping his hatchet to the floor.

Luke looked at the object in his hands, and realized that it was a revolver. The gun was fully-loaded with six .38 caliber rounds. He sighed with a breath of relief and tucked the revolver into the back of his pants.

"Let's get the locks off of those guns!" Scott said excitedly. He rushed out of the office and Luke followed, leaving the little hatchet behind.

When they emerged from the hallway, they found the other men still sleeping against the boxes. Scott picked up Sean's rifle first and tried one of the many keys on the big key ring. After several attempts, the lock popped open and fell off the trigger of the rifle to the floor.

"Good job," Luke commended Scott. Then he handed his double-barrel shotgun to Scott.

Scott used the same key on the shotgun's lock, and it opened on the first try. He handed the weapon back to Luke and picked up Joe's rifle.

Luke cradled the shotgun in both hands as if he was holding a baby. He held his shiny new weapon up, examining every inch of the beautiful gun. Gripping the shotgun with his right hand, he held his left wrist out and slapped the gun across his arm, opening the break-action on the barrels. He reached into his pocket and slid a shell into each of the chambers and clicked the action back into place with a snap of his wrist. He lifted the gun, aiming across the stockroom as he inspected the sights.

Meanwhile, Scott had unhooked the lock from Joe's rifle and was rousing the other men from their naps.

"You found the keys?" Sean asked sleepily.

"You bet," Scott replied with a smile. He tossed the unlocked rifle to Sean.

Sean and Joe loaded their rifles and inspected their new weapons, testing out the cocking mechanisms and looking through the sights.

"Looks like it's time for a shopping spree," Mark said, rubbing his eyes as he yawned.

Luke gave him a funny look, but the others smiled and nodded in agreement.

# 9

The five young men stood ready at the stockroom doors, armed with their new fully-loaded weapons. They had removed the barricade of boxes from in front of the doors and were waiting to see if the creatures were still lingering outside the doors.

"I don't hear anything," Joe said, looking down at the floor, his right ear facing the double-doors.

"They've probably spread out by now," Scott speculated. "If we make a run for it, I think we can make it to the shopping carts before they catch us."

"Let's go shopping!" Mark cried happily as he burst through the double-doors with a huge grin on his face.

Luke shook his head for a moment, pushing his glasses up on his nose. He took a deep breath and then joined the others in the charge. There were only a few zombies nearby, and their backs were turned to the men. By the time they turned around, the men had already passed by. The creatures were spread out, just as Scott had predicted.

When they reached the shopping carts at the front of the store, they noticed the glass doors at the front entrances were opening automatically, allowing the creatures to walk right into the store when they walked close enough to the motion-sensors above the doors.

"Damn it!" Scott cursed. "So that's how the bastards are getting inside!"

"Do you still have those keys?" Joe asked, peering through the scope on his rifle. He positioned the crosshairs on a nearby zombie's forehead and fired the first shot through his new rifle. His lips curled into a little smirk as the rifle butt kicked back into his shoulder. He watched through the scope as the bullet penetrated the creature's skull cleanly and its body collapsed to the floor.

"Right here," Scott replied, holding the large keychain up on his index finger. "You guys cover my ass good, okay? I'm going to lock those doors."

"Go for it," Sean said as he fired a bullet into the face of another creature. He cocked the lever on his rifle with a quick flick of his wrist, expelling the empty shell. He took careful aim at another zombie and blew a hole though its temple. Blood spurted out from the creature's head as it fell to the floor.

Scott rushed over to the automatic doors and leaned his shotgun against the wall. The doors opened as he approached, and another zombie walked into the store.

A bullet from Joe's rifle ripped through the creature's chest as soon as it entered through the doors. The zombie staggered for a moment and another bullet penetrated its skull, sending its body slamming to the floor below.

Scott flicked a power switch above the doors, turning off the motion sensor. He manually pushed the doors shut, but a creature's arm got caught between the doors, making it impossible to lock. He pushed as hard as he could to try and force the doors shut, but they just wouldn't budge. He looked over his shoulder, motioning to his friends for help.

Luke walked up to the entrance and lifted up his double-barrel shotgun, taking aim between the doors. He pressed the barrels against the zombie's head and fired, causing its head to explode. A shower of bright red blood drenched the glass doors.

Scott slammed the sliding doors shut and tried one of the keys on the lock. The first key didn't fit, so he tried another one. Luke rested his shotgun against the wall and helped Scott hold the doors shut. Just as a zombie emerged from behind the shopping carts next to Luke, Mark filled the creature's head with a hail of bullets. The zombie collapsed lifelessly to the floor at Luke's feet.

"It's not working," Scott said frantically as he tried to fit key after key into the lock.

"Keep trying!" Mark said, taking aim at another approaching creature. He fired two shots, but the bullets only penetrated walking corpse's chest, and it continued to advance on the young men. Mark squeezed the trigger again, but his handgun only made a clicking sound. He quickly pressed the magazine release button, and the empty clip ejected into his other hand. He fished around in his pocket for a moment, retrieved another loaded magazine, and popped it into his gun. Just as the approaching zombie got close enough to pose any immediate danger, Mark cocked the sliding mechanism on his gun and fired a shot. This time, the bullet struck the creature directly in the forehead, and it collapsed to the linoleum floor at Mark's feet.

Finally, the second-to-last key on Scott's keychain clicked into place, and he turned it, locking the doors. He breathed a sigh of relief, and removed the keys from the lock. He wiped the sweat from his brow with his sleeve.

Two more creatures appeared from the checkout lines, and Scott and Luke scrambled to get their shotguns.

Sean and Joe each fired their rifles, hitting both the zombies. One of the creatures fell as a bullet pierced its skull, but the other barely flinched as a bullet ripped though its neck. The zombie's head hung to one side, its neck damaged from the gunshot wound.

Scott cocked his shotgun and walked up to the zombie, aiming point-blank at its face.

"You dumb little bastard," Scott snarled. He fired his weapon and the creature's head ripped off in an explosion of blood and gore.

"There's another entrance over there," Luke said, pointing to the other side of the store.

Scott and Luke rushed toward the second entrance, dodging several creatures on their way. The other three men fired at the creatures in the way until the corpses dropped. Then the men joined Scott and Luke at the other entrance.

The second entrance was easier than the first, as there weren't as many zombies lingering around it. Luke held the doors shut and Scott quickly locked them.

The few creatures that still remained at the entrance were promptly shot by Sean, Joe and Mark. As the men stood in front of the locked doors catching their breath, a group of zombies began to gather outside the doors. They banged wildly on the glass, creating a loud ruckus. More creatures from the parking lot heard the noise and were attracted to the doors.

"That glass won't hold long," Mark said. He had popped the clip out of his Glock and was inserting bullets into it.

"That's okay," Scott said. "It should buy us enough time to gather the things we need."

Sean and Mark each grabbed a shopping cart. The others walked alongside them, shooting at the zombies that still remained in the store.

"I should have made a shopping list," Mark said, laughing.

"Let's just get what we need," Luke suggested, sighing.

"Let's get a microwave and some frozen food!" Sean said excitedly.

"I need a T.V. and some video games!" Joe chimed in.

"You guys go on ahead," Scott insisted, falling behind. "I'll catch up."

The other guys just nodded. They were too excited about their shopping spree to care. They started piling items into the shopping carts from every aisle they passed.

Sean headed straight for the frozen foods, stacking up T.V. dinners in his cart. Mark tossed a case of beer in his cart, and Joe emerged from the electronics department with a video game system and a stack of games. Luke added a large case of bottled water to the plunder.

Meanwhile, Scott had walked back to the front of the store. He headed straight for the checkout counter in the center of the store. He set his shotgun on the counter and reached behind the cigarette cabinet and grabbed a pack of Camel straights. As he turned, he spotted a shiny Zippo lighter on the other side of the counter and reached across to grab it.

Suddenly, a hand grabbed Scott's wrist. Scott leaned over the counter and looked down. On the floor, he saw a woman with long, blonde hair wearing a blue Wal-Mart uniform vest. The white shirt underneath her vest was drenched in dark blood, and her skin was as pale as death. In fact, she was one of the living dead. She held on tightly to Scott's wrist and took a huge bite of flesh from the top of his forearm as he screamed in agony.

"You bitch!" Scott cried, pulling his arm away. He scooped his shotgun up off the counter and pressed the barrel against the crown of zombie woman's head. He pulled the trigger, blasting a huge hole into the creature's skull, spewing blood and brain fragments all over the checkout counter and floor.

"Fuck you!" Scott yelled, spitting on the woman's corpse as he laid the shotgun back down on the counter. He ripped the blue vest off the woman's body and wrapped it tightly around the wound on his forearm, tying a knot with his other hand and pulling it tight with his teeth. He picked up his shotgun and grabbed a couple more packs of cigarettes, stuffing them in his pocket. As he turned to leave, he noticed a stack of cigarette cartons and scooped up as many as he could carry with one arm. He sighed deeply and walked off, disappearing into the aisles.

A little girl walked slowly across the main aisle from the toy section as she dragged a naked baby doll by its plastic arm along the shiny linoleum floor. The child was wearing a little pink dress with white polka dots, which was stained with streaks of dark crimson blood. Her skin had a light-gray tone to it with visible veins, and her eyes were vacant. As she turned the corner of the aisle, a large, gaping wound was visible on the right side of her neck. A loud gunshot rang out, and the little girl was blown backward into the air as a bullet penetrated her left shoulder. The undead child crashed into a nearby display of potato chips as her baby doll skidded across the tiles. She lay on the floor for a few seconds, staring blankly at the florescent lights overhead. She slowly began to stand back up, tilting her head to one side with her arms outstretched.

"You gotta aim for the head," Sean said, placing a hand on the smoking barrel of Joe's rifle. Sean lifted his own rifle and rested it on the handle of the shopping cart for added stability. He took careful aim through the scope, lining up the crosshairs between the little zombies eyes. As the creature staggered forward, he held his breath for a moment, squeezing the trigger slowly. The rifle fired a thunderous blast, and a bullet smashed through the creature's face. The little zombie froze in mid-stride, swaying from side to side before collapsing limply to the floor.

"Nice shot," Joe said, cocking the bolt on his rifle as an empty shell ejected from the chamber.

Mark returned from the wine aisle, carrying four bottles of expensive wine and a corkscrew. He placed three of the bottles in the shopping cart and popped the cork out of the remaining bottle. He tilted his head back, taking a big swig of the bottle, as some of the crimson liquid trickled down his cheeks.

Soon, the shopping carts were filled to the brim with food, gadgets, and goods from all over the store. Some of the items in the carts included a coffee pot, bags of fruit and vegetables, some bars of soap, bags of potato chips, toothbrushes, a box of plastic eating utensils, and several sticks of deodorant. Someone even managed to fit a mini-refrigerator in one of the carts.

"Let's try to hurry," Luke said nervously, fiddling with the shotgun shells in his pockets.

"Don't worry, buddy," Mark said, chuckling as he wiped the red liquid off of his face with his sleeve. "This place is ours now. Those creatures don't stand a chance."

Luke just shook his head slowly. His eyes darted from side to side, expecting something to go wrong at anytime.

Suddenly, a nearby clothing rack crashed to the floor, and a figure emerged from the aisle. Startled, Mark dropped his wine bottle and it crashed to the floor, breaking into pieces. Sean and Joe raised their rifles, ready to fire.

"Don't shoot," Scott said, raising his wounded arm. "It's me."

"Damn it, man!" Mark cried. "What the hell happened to you?" He rushed to his brother's side, staring at the blue cloth wrapped around Scott's arm, which was now soaked with fresh blood.

"It's okay," Scott said, dumping his collection of cigarette cartons into one of the shopping carts. "One of those things bit me, but I'm fine. It's just a small wound."

"Jesus Christ!" Luke exclaimed. "That's a lot of blood!"

"I said I'm fine!" Scott insisted. "Don't worry about it."

"We should probably stop by the first aid section," Sean suggested. "You need to take care of that arm."

"Yeah, yeah," Scott said, ripping open a pack of unfiltered Camels. He pulled a cigarette out of the pack with his mouth and lit it, taking a deep drag.

"I'll go," Mark volunteered. He grabbed a cigarette out of Scott's pack, and Scott lit it for him. "You guys go ahead and get this stuff to the stockroom. It's going to get dark soon, and those creatures seem to be more active at night."

"All right," Sean agreed. "But be careful." He slung his rifle over his shoulder and started pushing one of the shopping carts.

Luke took a deep breath, trying to calm his nerves. He realized that his hands were shaking, and he put his shotgun in the shopping cart next to Scott's cartons of cigarettes. He opened one of the cartons, retrieving a pack of cigarettes, and ripped it open. He put a cigarette in his mouth, even though he didn't smoke, and Scott lit it for him. He coughed several times as he inhaled the thick, unfiltered smoke.

"Let's go," Joe said, pushing the cart behind Sean.

The four young men returned to the stockroom, and Joe and Sean started unpacking their newly acquired goods while they waited for Mark to return. Scott opened a bottle of wine and sat against a stack of boxes, sipping from the bottle. As Scott sat watching the others, Luke paced anxiously at the double-doors, guarding the entrance to the stockroom as he held his double-barrel shotgun in both hands.

"Why don't you relax?" Scott said, leaning his head back against a box as he took a drag from his cigarette.

Luke stopped pacing for a moment and looked over at Scott. He glanced out through the small rectangular windows on the double-doors, and walked over to where Scott was sitting.

"Give me a sip," Luke insisted, reaching out his hand. Scott handed him the wine bottle and Luke took a huge gulp. He gave the bottle back to Scott and walked back to the doors.

Sean opened a large box in one of the shopping carts and lifted a brand-new microwave out of it. He placed it on top of a stack of boxes near the wall and plugged it into an electrical outlet.

"Who's hungry?" Sean asked with a smile.

"Me!" Joe exclaimed as he rummaged through the pile of T.V. dinners that Sean had brought back with them. He handed a box of macaroni and cheese to Sean.

"We've got company," Luke announced, peering through the little windows on the door.

Scott stood up with his shotgun in one hand and a cigarette dangling from his mouth. He took another swig of his wine, and cocked the pump on his shotgun.

"Is it Mark?" Joe asked, reaching for his rifle.

"No," Luke replied. "A couple of those creatures are headed this way."

Sean joined Luke at the double-doors. He peered out through one of the small windows and spotted a female zombie dressed in a jogging suit. To her right, a short, fat zombie man waddled slowly toward the stockroom.

"Take care of them," Sean said as the microwave beeped, signaling that the food was ready. "I'll throw another dinner in the microwave."

Luke kicked the doors open and took a few steps forward. He aimed his double-barrel shotgun in the middle of the two creatures as they staggered close to each other. He fired two consecutive shots, and the spray of lead smashed into both of the zombies' torsos. The creatures fell flat on their backs from the force of the blasts, but their heads were unscathed.

Scott stepped out in front while Luke reloaded. He lifted his pump-action weapon with one arm, aiming it at the male zombie as it tried to stand back up. He blasted a shot at the creature's face, and the zombie's head snapped back, smashing into the hard floor. The zombie lay motionless, its brain destroyed.

Joe put a hand on Scott's shoulder, holding up his rifle with his other hand. He took aim as Scott stepped back to give him space. He waited a moment for the female zombie to stand up, and fired a deafening shot, piercing her skull just below the nose. The creature's jaw dropped open, spewing blood onto the floor. Its lifeless body dropped to its knees before collapsing face-first onto the tile floor.

"Nice shot," Sean said, poking his head through the double-doors.

The sound of footsteps echoed through the nearby aisles, and the men tensed up, raising their weapons.

"I'm back," Mark said as he walked around the corner. He was carrying a box of bandages and several bottles of ointment.

Joe ejected an empty shell from his rifle and quickly clicked the bolt back into place. He aimed the rifle toward Mark, and Mark dropped what he was carrying, ducking to the floor.

"What the hell?" Mark cried as he looked up in surprise at Joe, who was aiming the rifle over his head.

Joe fired a shot as a creature dropped to the floor directly behind where Mark had been standing.

"Thanks, man," Mark gasped, sighing a breath of relief as his ears rang from the loud gunshot. He picked up the box of bandages, and his brother scooped up the bottles of ointment.

"We'd better barricade the doors again," Joe suggested. "There's no telling how many of those things are still in the store."

The others agreed, and they made another stack of boxes at the doors inside the stockroom. As they sat around eating the T.V. dinners that Sean had cooked, Scott removed the blood-soaked cloth from his forearm and applied some antibacterial ointment to his wound. Mark helped him wrap one of the bandages around his arm.

After dinner, the men sat around for several hours drinking wine and smoking cigarettes as they discussed their situation. The Walker brothers were adamant about setting up house inside the store. They were very optimistic about their chance of survival if they stayed at the store, although Mark was somewhat concerned about his brother's arm. Sean and Joe were slightly less enthusiastic about the idea of boxing themselves up inside the large building, but they didn't put up much of an argument against the plan. Luke, on the other hand, was very opposed.

"We need to take what we can and get the hell out of here before it's too late!" Luke cried, fed up with the Walker brothers' suggestions to turn the store into a fortress of survival. He had heard enough of their crazy plans.

"Trust me," Scott said, taking a drag from his cigarette and blowing smoke out of his nostrils. "We'll last a lot longer in here than out there. Where the hell are you suggesting we go?"

"Jacksonville," Luke replied without a second thought.

"You're crazy!" Mark blurted out, as Joe and Sean snickered.

"There's bound to be more survivors in the big city," Luke said pleadingly.

"And a hell of a lot more zombies!"

"But they have more military and police to deal with them. They've got to have a lot of rescue stations over there."

"If they're anything like the one we came from," Scott butted in, "we'd be crazy to go there. Those rescue stations are madhouses."

"And we have things in control here," Mark added. "We can deal with this much better on our own."

"I bet the people back at that rescue station would die if they knew what we have here," Scott said, smirking.

"Yeah," Luke agreed sarcastically. "And they'd probably kill to have what we've got, too. That's another thing I'm worried about."

"Stop worrying," Mark said, putting his hand on Luke's shoulder as he took a sip from his wine bottle. "We can deal with those creatures, and we can deal with looters. We have so many guns and so much ammo in here they would have to send the army to get into this place."

"We've got everything we could ever dream of having right here," Scott added. "And I'm in no hurry to leave anytime soon."

Luke looked over at Sean and Joe who were quietly nodding their heads in agreement.

"You guys are brainwashed by this place," Luke said, throwing his hands up in the air. He finished his last drop of wine and threw the empty bottle across the room in anger. He grabbed another bottle and stormed off down the hallway into the shadows.

Joe and Sean sat quietly drinking their wine, staring at the Walker brothers.

"He'll get over it," Mark said, standing up. He dropped his cigarette butt, stomped on it, and walked to the restroom, shutting the door behind him.

"In the meantime," Scott said, finishing the last sip of his wine, "I'm going to get some sleep." He leaned against a stack of boxes, closing his eyes.

"Maybe tomorrow we can get some beds from the furniture department," Sean suggested.

"Good idea," Joe said. "It'd be nice to get some real sleep around here."

The two men moved some boxes against the wall, creating makeshift beds, and laid down on them. Mark returned from the restroom after a few minutes, and soon, all the men were sound asleep—all of them except for Luke, of course.

The skinny black-haired man was sitting at the desk in the center of another room, chain-smoking as he polished off another bottle of wine. His hair was a matted mess, and beads of sweat lined his forehead. The room around him was filled with black and white television screens, which displayed views of every inch of the store from the multitude of security cameras. His eyes were fixed on two particular screens, which showed an overhead view of the front entrances to the store.

The creatures outside the entrances were still banging relentlessly on the glass, adamant in their attempts to get inside the store. They were either hungry for the warm, living flesh of the five survivors, or they just wanted to be inside the store–a significant place from their former lives.

Luke watched as the army of zombies continued to increase in number before his very eyes. The racket from the creatures that were pounding on the entrance attracted more and more ghouls that had been wondering aimlessly in the parking lot. Zombies of all shapes and sizes staggered slowly toward the entrances from the vast parking lot.

"The bastards won't stop until they get in," Luke mumbled to himself, taking a big guzzle of wine. He slammed the bottle down onto the desk, wiping the red liquid off his chin without taking an eye off the television monitors. He leaned back in the desk chair, feeling the effects of the alcohol pulse through his head. He put another cigarette in his mouth, lighting it with the one he just finished, and flicked the finished butt to the floor. He sat still for a few minutes, scanning the security monitors.

Then it dawned on him. He remembered the hardware section of the store. It had all sorts of tools and supplies! Something clicked in his brain as he glanced back at the monitors showing the front doors. They could board up the entrance to the store! They had everything that they would need right there at their fingertips!

No, he thought, pounding his fist onto the desk as his glasses slipped down his nose. Don't start thinking like *them*. They wouldn't be blocking the creatures from getting inside—they would be imprisoning themselves inside a concrete tomb! He had to keep his head on straight. Taking another gulp of wine, he pushed his glasses up and glared at the mob of ghouls on the television screens.

But then again, where else *would* they go? The Walker brothers did have a point. Maybe the best thing that they could do was to try and survive with what they had. And there were so many things in the store that they could use.

There was no way they could take everything with them. Their vehicles could only hold so much.

It just might work. But they would have to be smart and keep their heads together. If they worked together to secure the place, they just might have a chance at survival.

Luke watched the creatures on the television monitors as they tried in vain to get through the glass doors. He took a deep drag from his cigarette, the corners of his mouth curling up with a slight smirk. He leaned back in the chair, propping his feet up on the desk, letting the cigarette hang from his mouth.

Samantha sat quietly reading a psychology textbook by the candlelight, oblivious to the loud banging on the metal trailer walls. She twirled a lock of her long, black hair between her fingers as she read, deeply engrossed in a theory of human needs. As she turned the page of her textbook, the sudden crash of glass breaking startled her from her deep thoughts.

"Jesus!" the young woman cried as her heart skipped a beat. The book fell off her lap to the carpet floor.

"I got it," a gruff voice called out from down the hall.

Charlie emerged from the bedroom and peered out through the shattered window in the hall. Horrible moans became audible, leaking in through the newly open portal from the darkness outside.

The young woman picked up her book off the floor, dusting it off as she watched the tall, burly man press a thick board across the window frame.

"Don't worry," the big man said as he hammered a nail into the board, pinning it firmly to the wall. "They can't get in."

"I know, Charlie," the woman replied. "And we can't get out."

The husky man sighed and drove another nail into the board. A pale hand reached over the top of the board, grabbing Charlie's hand, but he quickly smashed his hammer into the cold hand, shattering its finger bones. The hand quickly retracted back through the window opening.

"Samantha," the big man called out, looking over to the young woman, who was coiled up comfortably in a recliner. "Can you give me a hand over here?"

The woman sighed and rested her book on the coffee table. She walked over to the big man's side in the narrow hallway. She held the board up with both hands as he drove another nail into place.

"Thanks, sweetie," the large man said, resting the hammer on the floor under the window. He put a huge arm around Samantha and kissed her on the cheek.

"How much longer will power be out?" the petite woman asked, returning Charlie's hug.

"No idea," the big man replied, scratching the back of his neck. "We'll just have to wait and see."

The young couple had been living in the small trailer without electricity for several days. They had survived against the small horde of undead that had surrounded the little trailer by boarding up the windows and keeping the doors locked. Although the trailer was parked in the middle of the woods off of a dirt road, far away from the big city, the ghouls had somehow managed to find them. The couple had been listening to the radio each day, which had been broadcasting brief announcements at random intervals, until the batteries had finally run out. Now they were stuck in the middle of nowhere, surrounded by a small army of walking corpses. They had a small amount of canned food left, and most of the food in the refrigerator had begun to go bad since the electricity had been off for several days. They still had running water, however, and water came from a well.

Charlie took Samantha by the hand, and they walked into the living room. The room was lit up by the eerie glow of candlelight. They could hear the creatures outside moaning, hungry for the warm flesh of the survivors inside. The big man sat down in the recliner, pulling Samantha into his lap.

"We can't stay here forever," he said, looking her in the eyes.

"I know," she returned, nodding her head as she stared at his stubble-covered face.

"I have a half-tank of gas in my truck," he said.

Samantha combed her fingers through her long, dark hair, as several silky locks fell across her face.

"Those things out there…" Charlie continued. "They move around so slow. I'm pretty sure we can slip right past 'em."

The thin woman chewed on her thumbnail, staring blankly across the room.

"Sam?" the big man said, placing a hand on his girlfriend's shoulder.

"I don't want to go," Samantha said, looking back into Charlie's eyes as she shook her head. Her tanned skin seemed to glow in the candlelight as she stood up off the big man's lap. She walked into the kitchen and opened up the pantry door.

There was a small stack of canned soup and some vegetables on the bottom shelf. Besides the single opened box of wheat crackers that stood on the middle ledge, the other shelves were barren.

"We've got to survive," Charlie said as he walked up behind Samantha, curling his arms around her belly as he hugged her from behind. "We just can't stay here."

"I like it here," the young woman said.

"We can't last much longer here."

"We've done fine so far."

The big man grabbed the opened box of crackers and dumped the contents onto the kitchen counter. He took a small handful of broken crackers and shoveled them into his mouth.

"We need food," he said, leaning his elbows on the counter.

The young woman sighed, looking down at the floor thoughtfully.

"If we get food, can we come back here?" she asked as she placed a hand on the large man's shoulder.

"Maybe...we'll see how things work out."

"I just can't imagine where we would go."

"I'm sorry, honey. But we have no choice."

Samantha sighed and crossed her arms.

"We'll figure something out," the brawny man assured her.

The next morning, Charlie woke up at the crack of dawn. He lay in bed for a few minutes, watching Samantha as she slept. Even though her hair was matted and she had not bathed for days, she looked beautiful to him. He kissed her softly on the forehead and got out of bed.

The power was still off.

He picked up the telephone, but there was still no dial tone, just as he had suspected. Replacing the receiver on the hook, he peered through a crack between some boards on the window. There were more creatures in the yard. One of the ghouls looked like his neighbor from down the road, Mr. Johnson, but it was hard to tell. The creature's face was caked with dried blood from a gaping wound on its forehead, and its clothes had been ripped to shreds.

Charlie walked into the kitchen and turned on the gas stove. He lit a match and a blue flame ignited underneath one of the burners. He opened the last can of vegetable soup and dumped it into the pot.

The banging sounds started again from the front of the trailer, and Charlie tensed up. He just couldn't get used to the relentless racket that the horrible creatures constantly produced. He rushed to the corner of the living room and picked up the hunting rifle that was propped against the wall. Cocking the bolt on the gun, he peered out through a space between the wooden planks on the front window. The glass had been broken out several nights before, and the cool morning air leaked through the opening.

"Shut the hell up!" Charlie yelled angrily as he spotted one of the creatures pounding on the metal wall. He poked the barrel of the rifle through the crack in the window and lined it up with the creature's head. He fired a single shot, and the creature dropped.

Samantha's eyes popped open at the sound of the gunshot. She sat up quickly in bed, wrapped in a tangle of blankets.

"Charlie?" she called out concertedly.

"I'm here," the muffled reply came from the living room.

"You okay in there?"

"I'm fine."

She laid her head back down on the pillow, staring blankly at the idle ceiling fan.

The big man entered the room, rifle in hand.

"It's time to go, honey," he said softly.

Samantha rolled over in bed.

"We can't stay here any longer," he added. He walked over to the edge of the bed and reached his hand out to her.

The young woman sighed, grabbing her boyfriend's hand as he pulled her gently up out of bed. She reached into the dresser and stuffed some clothes into a purple backpack on the floor. The young couple walked into the kitchen and gathered up the small amount of remaining food into a grocery bag.

"Got everything?" the big man asked as he picked up his rifle, slinging a large sack over his shoulder.

"Yep," Samantha replied, standing anxiously by the door. "Oh, wait!" She scurried over to the coffee table and stuffed her psychology textbook into her backpack.

"All right," Charlie said, taking a deep breath. "Let's go!" He picked up the keys to the truck from a hook on the wall and put his hand on the doorknob. Hesitating for moment at the door, he waited for his girlfriend to join him.

Samantha got behind Charlie, placing a hand on his back for support as she waited. The big man abruptly swung the door open, ramming it forcefully into a creature that had been standing outside. The ghoul flew backward, landing on the far end of the wooden porch.

"Go, Charlie, go!" Samantha yelled from inside the doorway.

Two creatures stood in front of the brown pickup truck facing the couple. The big man walked down the stairs toward one of the slow-moving corpses and slammed the butt of his rifle into its face. The ghoul fell back, crashing into the hood of the truck. Its body slid down the grill to the dirt below.

Samantha jumped off the porch, making a dash for the passenger door of the truck, as Charlie aimed his semi-automatic rifle toward the other zombie at close-range. He fired two consecutive shots, and the creature dropped.

"Hurry, Charlie!" the young woman cried, pulling on the handle of the door on the truck. Frantically, she lifted the handle several times, but the locked door wouldn't budge.

Charlie rushed around the front of the truck and unlocked the passenger door. The young woman hastily tossed her backpack into the cab and jumped inside, locking the door behind her.

Suddenly, the big man felt a cold hand on his shoulder, and he spun around. A badly disfigured female corpse stepped out from the bushes, one of its eyeballs hanging loosely from its socket. Charlie pushed the creature away with one hand and the creature stumbled back into the bushes, but it bounced right back at him. The beast crashed into the big man's chest, knocking him backward against the hood of the truck. He lost his grip on the rifle, and it fell from his hand, rolling into the bushes.

"Charlie!" the woman screamed from inside the vehicle. She watched helplessly through the windshield of the truck as the horror unfolded in front of her.

The creature clawed at the man with its long, filthy fingernails as it lay on top of him. The horrible stench of the moving corpse caused Charlie to choke. The beast opened its mouth to bite him, but he held it back with the palm of his hand, its long fingernails clawing into the flesh on his arms.

Samantha struggled to open the door, forgetting that she had locked it. As she banged on the glass window, she caught a glimpse of another creature that stumbled around the corner of the trailer, drooling as it stretched its arms out toward the commotion in the driveway. In frenzy, the young woman unlocked the passenger door and jumped out, grabbing the female zombie by the arm. She tugged as hard as she could, and the creature turned its head to face her.

Charlie smashed his powerful fist into the ghoul's jaw and it tumbled off of him, crashing into Samantha.

Suddenly, the other zombie grabbed Charlie's face with both of its hands, blinding the big man. It leaned down over the hood as Charlie thrashed his arms around, trying desperately to break free. In one quick motion, the creature snapped its rotting teeth down on him, biting a small chunk of flesh out of his neck.

"No!" the young woman screamed in horror.

Charlie cried out in pain as blood gushed onto the hood of the truck. He lifted the ghoul up with both hands as a sudden burst of adrenaline pulsed through his body, and hurled the creature through the air into the bushes. Then he grabbed the female zombie by its hair, jerking its neck back as he pulled it away from Samantha. He turned quickly, slamming the ghoul's face down violently onto the hood of the truck. The creature collapsed to the ground at his feet as he crushed its frail skull under the heel of his boot. He lifted his foot, staggering backward as a sudden wave of dizziness consumed him.

"Charlie!" Samantha screamed as her eyes filled with tears.

"I need you to drive," the big man gasped, clutching the wound on his neck as blood spilled down onto his shirt.

"We've got to take care of that…"

"Just do it!"

Samantha helped Charlie into the passenger seat, her hands trembling. She slid over top of him onto the driver's side and started the engine. She threw it in reverse and turned around to look back just as another ghoul started banging against the driver-side window.

The truck peeled out in reverse down the driveway in a cloud of dust, leaving the small group of creatures behind. Samantha stomped on the gas, and the truck sped off down the dusty dirt road.

Charlie ripped his flannel shirt open and took it off. He tied it around his neck, covering his open wound. Blood oozed through the cloth, but it slowed the bleeding.

"I'm going to find help," Samantha said, her voice cracking.

"I'll be all right," the big man gasped, clenching his teeth. "Just get us out of here."

The truck barreled down the dirt road through the woods with none of the creatures in sight for several miles. Soon, they reached the main road. It was an old country road in the middle of nowhere, but at least it was paved. The young woman turned the corner sharply, heading west as they passed a sign that read: "Tallahassee—26 miles."

They had left the rifle behind, but Samantha didn't even think about it. Her only thought was to find help for her injured boyfriend. Her heart pounded in her chest as she drove faster and faster toward the city.

The large man in the passenger seat moaned in agony, writhing back and forth with each bump in the road.

"Don't worry, baby," the young woman said, placing her softly hand on the man's wrist. "It's not much farther." She tried to stay calm, but her mind was racing. She felt a wave of panic coming on, and her hands began to shake uncontrollably. She pulled her arm away, hoping Charlie wouldn't notice. Taking a deep breath, she exhaled through her mouth, trying to calm herself.

She turned on the radio and the speakers hissed with static. She tuned the dial, but none of the stations were broadcasting. Unable to get a signal, she clicked the power button off and continued driving in silence.

Twenty minutes passed, and she began to notice more creatures as they drew closer to the outskirts of town. As she approached a gas station, she eased up on the gas, slowing down a little as she spotted a pillar of smoke rising from the parking lot. An overturned car blocked the entrance, and a small group of people was crowded around it.

She tapped the brakes, slowing down almost to a stop, hoping that the people might be able to help her. Driving closer, her heart sunk as she recognized that the people were, in fact, not human. Their skin was pale and their mouths were covered with blood. They were feeding on a dead body that was hanging halfway out of the window of the overturned car. The ghouls were ripping out strings of bloody intestines from the mutilated body, gnawing viciously on the tender morsels of human tissue. Holding back a wave of nausea, Samantha stomped on the gas, speeding off down the road.

Charlie was quiet. He hadn't spoken a word since they had left the countryside.

"How are you holding up?" the young woman asked.

The big man groaned, shifting in the seat.

"I'm making it," he gruffly replied. Charlie had been caught up in his world of pain, unaware of what had been going on around him for the past half-hour. The bleeding had slowed, and he sat up halfway in the seat, looking around.

"Take it easy, baby," Samantha said, putting her hand on Charlie's leg.

"Where's the rifle?" he asked, his eyes darting around the cab.

Samantha thought for a moment, her mind racing again. Then she remembered.

"We left it in the yard."

"Damn it!" the big man cursed, hitting the dashboard with an open hand.

"Careful, honey," Samantha said with concern. "Don't hurt yourself."

Charlie sat silently, but Samantha could sense his rage.

"It's gonna be okay," she said calmingly, trying to convince herself that it would be.

The old pickup truck gained speed steadily as it raced toward the city limits. Soon, the distant skyline of the city became visible on the horizon, and the sun shined brightly overhead through the cool morning air. The small, two-lane country road had transitioned to a four-lane highway, but it was devoid of any other vehicles. The rural, natural scenery was replaced by concrete sidewalks lined with streetlamps, gas stations, and small shopping centers. Old newspapers, empty soda cans, and other random trash was strewn about on the sidewalks and parking lots.

Samantha had to swerve to avoid the hordes of walking corpses that were milling about through the streets and sidewalks. Their horrible moans became audible as the truck passed by them. Samantha had to slow down to avoid crashing into the creatures.

She glanced down at the gas gauge. The needle hovered just above quarter of a tank marker. Her heart began to race as she looked back up, scanning the area around them. The truck was surrounded by the creatures, but it continued to press forward at a moderate pace. She steered the wheel to the left and right, weaving in and out between the living dead. The old truck smashed into several of the creatures, unable to avoid them, catapulting their bodies high into the air. But the heavy truck kept moving forward, virtually unscathed by the frail, rotting bodies of the hideous ghouls.

"Where can we go?" the young woman frantically asked as a panic began to envelop her again. Her hands were shaking as she gripped tightly onto the steering wheel. She braced herself as the truck smashed head-on into another ghoul, its bones crunching beneath the wheels.

"Over there!" the big man exclaimed, pointing to a large sign ahead on the opposite side of the road.

Samantha turned the wheel sharply, steering into the opposite lane. She turned again and the truck raced through the entrance under the sign into a massive parking lot.

Charlie grunted as the truck barreled across a speedbump. The bloody shirt came loose from his neck, but he caught it, pulling it tight again. He slouched down in the seat as the truck crashed through a small army of zombies. The windshield cracked, forming a bulge in the glass as the head of a creature propelled into it, leaving a splatter of red blood behind.

As the truck roared noisily through the parking lot, more ghouls took notice of the vehicle. They careened slowly across the concrete landscape, hungry for the flesh of the passengers inside.

"Hold on, Charlie," the young woman gasped, slamming on the brakes as the trucks wheels slid into a screeching U-turn. The old vehicle skidded to a sudden stop near the entrance to the parking lot, facing the large superstore at the end of the lot. She put it in first gear and revved the engine as the roaring sound echoed across the parking lot. She sat still for a moment with her hands grasping tightly on the wheel, her wide eyes fixed firmly ahead. Her chest rose and fell rapidly as the tension built in her nerves.

"Here we go!" she cried, lifting her foot off the clutch.

**Nathan Tucker**

# 11

"What the hell are we gonna do?" someone yelled frantically, the words shaking Mark from his deep sleep.

Mark opened his eyes quickly, startled and half-awake. His heart pounded rhythmically in his chest.

"They're looters, I know it!" Joe cried, his back turned to where Mark lay.

"What's going on?" Mark demanded, sitting up on the stack of boxes where his pistol rested.

"There's a truck out there!" Sean exclaimed, pointing toward the barricaded double-doors.

"Out where?" Mark asked as he stood up, grabbing his gun.

"In the parking lot," Joe answered. "They're driving around out there."

"Where the hell are Scott and Luke?" Mark inquired, rubbing the sleep from his eyes.

Sean and Joe pointed down the hallway toward the room with the security monitors, and Mark ran toward the door.

"Look, man," Scott said to Luke as he sat on the edge of the desk, staring at a T.V. screen. "It's no big deal. We can deal with one car."

Luke bit his fingernails as he watched the vehicle barrel across the parking lot, crashing into several ghouls as their bodies catapulted into the air.

"Hey," Mark said as he entered the room. "What's going on?"

"It's just a small truck," Scott said, turning his head to greet his brother.

"How many people are in there?" Mark asked, his eyes narrowing as he looked up at the monitors.

"Can't tell," Luke replied. "It's moving too fast."

Suddenly, the truck skidded to a stop at the far end of the parking lot. It sat still for a moment, and the three men watching the monitors began to wander what had happened. Then its tires screeched on the pavement as smoke rose behind the car. It barreled off through the parking lot, heading straight for the main entrance of the store.

"What the hell are they doing?" Scott cried as he watched in horror as the vehicle picked up speed, smashing through a group of ghouls that were crowded around the entrance.

The vehicle crashed violently through the glass doors as an avalanche of glass shards crashed to the ground. It came to a stop as it collided into a collection of shopping carts. The hood of the truck crunched up in a contorted mass of metal as several shopping carts flew into the air, landing several yards away.

Scott stared at the monitors in disbelief as a horde of zombies began to pour in through the compromised entrance. Angrily, he picked up his shotgun off the desk and stormed out of the room as a wave of adrenaline rushed through his veins.

Mark and Luke stood gazing at the monitors for a moment, and then followed Scott into the stockroom.

"What was that noise?" Sean asked as he and Joe stood in front of the barricade of boxes, cradling their rifles.

"They broke through," Scott replied, pumping his shotgun.

Mark and Luke scurried to the stack of boxes and helped Scott as they removed the barricade. They pushed the last box out of the way, and Scott swung the double-doors open with the butt of his shotgun.

As the group of five ran toward the front of the store, they were greeted by a mob of zombies. Beyond the group of creatures sat the smashed up pickup truck, covered in broken glass. Several ghouls surrounded the vehicle, prying at the doors as they beat on the windows.

"Let's hold our ground here," Scott said, stopping in mid-stride about a hundred feet away from the truck. He lifted his shotgun, firing at the crowd of zombies as they approached. One of the ghouls at the front of the pack dropped to the floor as the others stepped over its body.

Mark fired again and again into the mob, some of his bullets reaching their target, and some of them passing harmlessly through limbs and torsos of the undead. Several zombies collapsed as blood spilled onto the floor from their heads.

Sean and Joe stood behind the Walker brothers, firing carefully-aimed shots into the horde, while Luke faced the opposite direction and guarded his comrades' backs with his shotgun.

As the size of the small army of undead began to decrease, the driver's door of the truck suddenly swung open, crashing into a passing zombie. A young woman stepped out of the truck. Her long, black hair fluttered in the breeze blowing through the compromised entrance.

Sean fired a well-aimed shot at the zombie closest to the woman, and the bullet penetrated the creature's skull.

"Stay where you are!" Scott ordered the woman. He blasted a shot into a nearby zombie as he walked cautiously toward the woman. He cocked his shotgun, expelling an empty shell, and pointed the gun at the woman.

"Don't shoot!" she cried, raising her hands frantically. "My boyfriend is hurt!"

"What the hell were you thinking?" Scott asked, noticing the large man leaning back in the passenger seat of the truck. He cast his gaze over at the front entrance to the store, surveying the damage. Almost all of the glass was now gone, laying in pieces on the floor, and more zombies were shuffling in from the parking lot.

"Please," the woman pleaded, her eyes welling up with tears. "We need help."

The other young men walked up behind Scott, firing random shots at creatures entering the store.

"My boyfriend was bitten by one of those monsters," she continued, her voice cracking. "He needs help."

Scott paused, keeping his shotgun trained on the young woman. He thought for a moment, glancing back at his friends. Then he turned back around, his face turning red.

"You dumb bitch!" he yelled, shaking his gun at the woman as she cowered back in fear. "You opened a fucking hole in the store! What the hell is wrong with you?"

"Please!" the woman cried, holding her hands out as she dropped to her knees. "I'm sorry!"

Sean and Joe lowered their rifles and rushed to the woman's side, but Scott stayed where he was standing, his face flushed with anger. Mark and Luke walked around the truck, firing at several wandering zombies.

"It's all right," Joe said, placing a hand on the woman's shoulder.

"What's your name?" Sean asked.

"Samantha," the woman replied, wiping the tears from her eyes.

"All right, Samantha," Sean said, slinging his rifle over his shoulder. "My name is Sean, and this is Joe. Let's have a look at your man, okay?"

The woman rushed around the truck and opened the passenger door, and the two young men followed her.

Scott shook his head angrily, pulling a cigarette out of his pocket. He lit it, blowing the smoke from the corner of his mouth as he glared at the young woman.

"How's it going in there?" Sean asked, sticking his head into the truck.

The man inside groaned as he pressed a blood-soaked cloth against his neck.

Sean stepped back, giving Joe a look of uncertainty.

Joe nodded, taking the woman gently by the arm as he led her away from the truck. "It's going to be okay," he assured her as he walked her over to a nearby cooler full of sodas and bottled water. "Don't worry about Scott. He'll cool off."

Mark and Luke fired their weapons again, felling several more zombies that had stumbled into the store, and the woman tensed up for a moment.

"We're going to need more bandages," Sean said to no one in particular. "And maybe we should check out that pharmacy." He pointed to the pharmacy in front of the checkout stands, which was blocked off by a roll-down gate.

"What are we gonna do about the entrance?" Scott asked with a tone of anger in his voice. He took a drag from his cigarette, letting the smoke bellow from his open mouth.

"We can deal with it," Sean replied as he pushed a shopping cart next to the truck. "Help me out here. Grab his legs."

Scott rested his shotgun against the hood of the truck and helped Sean lift the big man onto the shopping cart. The man groaned in agony as they laid him in the cart.

"I'll get him to the stockroom," Sean said. "Can you handle the rest?"

"Yeah," Scott replied, sighing. "I got it." He lifted his shotgun, blasting a nearby zombie away, and walked over to where Joe and Samantha were standing, drinking some water. Samantha lowered her head as Scott approached.

"We should probably get back the stockroom," Scott suggested, grabbing a soda from the cooler. He pointed over his shoulder at the increasing number of zombies that were now entering the store. As he turned, he rolled his eyes at the young woman.

"All right," Joe agreed, patting Samantha on the back. "Let's go."

Mark and Luke lingered behind for a few minutes while the others walked quickly to the back of the store. The two men stood side-by-side, firing at the creatures that were entering the store, until the numbers of the undead began to overwhelm them. Soon, they made a hasty retreat back to the stockroom, followed closely by a slow-moving army of the walking dead. They replaced the barrier of boxes at the double-doors just as the horde of monsters caught up to them.

In the stockroom, Samantha had dressed her boyfriend's wound and replaced the bloody shirt on his neck with some bandages that Mark had given her. She was holding a bottle of water up to the man's mouth as he lay on a stack of boxes. The big man took several gulps of the cold liquid, coughing in small fits as he drank.

"We'll have to board up the entrances," Luke said, leaning against the concrete wall as he stroked his goatee.

"Aren't you the one who wanted to leave?" Scott blurted out as he sat on a box.

"I've been thinking," Luke said, crossing his arms. He hesitated for a moment, trying to find the words. "Maybe you were right. We have everything we need right here. And we could board up those entrances easily with all the stuff in the hardware section."

The big man cried out in agony, tossing and turning on the makeshift bed.

"I'm here, Charlie," Samantha said soothingly as she hugged the man, laying her head on his chest.

Scott gazed at the blood-soaked bandages on the husky man's neck. Then he looked down at his own wounded arm, rubbing it softly. The pain had gotten worse, but Scott wasn't one to complain.

"We're gonna have to get some medicine," Scott said, looking over at Luke as he walked to the mini-fridge. He opened it, grabbed two beers, and tossed one to Luke.

Mark, Joe, and Sean had opened a pack of playing cards and were dealing a hand of poker in the corner of the room.

"There's another set of keys in the security room," Luke said as the opened his bottle of beer. "I'll bet the key to the pharmacy is in there."

The two men walked down the hallway toward the little room. Inside, Luke pulled the keys off a hook on the wall and strummed through them. Sure enough, one of the keys had a little white label on it that read, "Pharmacy." He tossed the keychain to Scott.

Scott's eyes lit up with excitement as he caught the keys.

"So…" Joe said, looking over his shoulder at Samantha as he dealt a hand of poker to Sean and Mark. "Where are you guys from?"

"Outside Monticello," the young woman replied as she soaked up the sweat from Charlie's forehead with a washcloth.

"Out in the sticks, eh?"

"Yeah… out in the sticks."

"How's your man doing?"

"He's holding up."

Joe tossed his cards on the table, folding his hand. He got up and grabbed a beer from the little refrigerator as Scott and Luke emerged from the hallway.

"I'll be back," Scott said as he grabbed his shotgun.

"Where you headed?" Mark asked, looking up from his cards.

"I'm gonna check out the pharmacy," Scott replied as he loaded a shell into his gun.

"You need any help?" Sean asked.

"Nah, I'll be fine." As Scott started removing some of the boxes from the double-doors, the doors suddenly swung open. A collage of hands reached through the doorway and Scott jumped back out of their reach.

The other young men sprang into action as a flood of zombies charged into the stockroom. The men quickly grabbed their weapons, and the room lit up with the flashes of their gunfire.

Samantha screamed, instinctively hovering over her injured boyfriend to protect him. She flinched as the loud shots exploded around her in a series of rapid bursts.

The creatures fell one by one as Scott blasted his shotgun again and again, pumping it quickly between each shot. His brother stood behind him, firing the Glock over his shoulder while Sean and Joe picked the creatures off with well-aimed shots from their rifles. Luke knelt on the floor nearby, discharging his double-barrel shotgun into the swarm, hitting multiple ghouls with each burst of fire.

The battle was over almost as quickly as it had begun. An eerie silence filled the room as the last creature hit the floor. The entrance was now littered with the corpses of fallen zombies.

The five men stood speechless for a moment, crouched down and ready for action, as smoke rose from the barrels of their guns.

"Holy...*Jesus!*" Mark exclaimed as he chuckled in astonishment. His heart still pounded excitedly in his chest. The overwhelming firepower that the young men now possessed literally amazed him.

"I might need a little help after all," Scott said, laughing as he lowered his weapon. He had already forgotten about the front entrance, and he slapped himself on the forehead for not remembering.

"I'll go with you," Samantha volunteered as she stood up.

Scott glanced over at the young woman and wrinkled his brow at her.

"No way," he said, shaking his head.

"Charlie needs some painkillers. I'm going with you."

"I'll bring him some."

"I'm not totally helpless, you know! I know how to shoot a gun."

"You're not going. Stay here with your man."

"Don't worry," Sean said as he loaded his rifle. "We'll be back soon."

"You're not leaving me without a gun!" Samantha demanded.

"I'll stay with her," Joe offered.

"I can protect myself!" the young woman exclaimed. "Just give me a damn gun!"

The five young men looked at each other for a moment.

"We'll get you one," Sean said. "We'll drop by the Sporting Goods on our way back."

Samantha glanced at Sean for a moment, and then turned her attention back to Scott.

"Just get the pills for Charlie," she pleaded. "Please..."

The annoyed look on Scott's face morphed into an expression of sincerity. "I will," he assured her.

The four men turned and exited the stockroom. Joe stayed behind, and Samantha helped him replace the stack of crates at the doorway.

The young men stood outside the entrance to the stockroom, weapons in hand as they looked out into the store. From their vantage point, there were no creatures in sight.

"Well," Scott said, "let's make this quick." He dashed off through the aisles, and the other three followed him. As they approached the front of the store, they stopped in front of a large magazine rack, peering out across the checkout stands. There were a number of zombies lumbering about in the open area, but they were considerably spread out.

"The pharmacy is right over there," Scott whispered, pointing to the roll-down gate on the wall opposite the checkout stands.

Several zombies were rummaging mindlessly through a candy bin in front of a checkout counter. They pawed curiously at the shiny packages of bubblegum and candy bars as melted chocolate oozed out onto their clothes. The creatures stumbled about, their simple brains too preoccupied to notice as the four young men snuck between a checkout line.

When the men reached the checkout counter, they ducked to the floor. Scott peeked around the corner and signaled that the coast was clear. The four men dashed across the storefront and slipped quietly into the women's restroom at the front wall. Scott ducked underneath a water fountain, waiting silently as a zombie trudged past the restrooms.

The men waited patiently as the sluggish creature stumbled off into the store.

"All right," Scott whispered. "Cover me good, you hear?" He tiptoed along the wall over to the front of the pharmacy, and the other men followed suit. When they reached the metal roll-down gate, the young men spread out. Mark knelt down on one side with his M-16 in hand, Sean stayed at the other side, and Luke guarded Scott's back as he unlocked the gate. The key clicked as it turned, and the gate loosened.

"Ready?" Scott asked, and the other men nodded. Slowly, he pulled the gate up as quietly as he could. The metal squeaked a little as the gate rose, but none of the ghouls noticed the sound.

It was considerably dark inside the pharmacy, but just enough light leaked through from the store for the men to see what they were doing. They walked through the small waiting room and hopped over the counter. The shelves behind the counter were stocked full of various pill bottles and jars of liquids. There was even a shelf with bags of filled prescriptions that hadn't been picked up by customers. The bags were labeled with the various names of customers who had filled out prescriptions weeks prior—before the world had gone mad. Other shelves were lined with name-brand drugs arranged in alphabetical order.

The men browsed curiously through the array of medical containers. Sean grabbed several bottles of various antibiotics and stuffed them in his pocket. Scott found two bottles that caught his attention—a container labeled "OxyContin," and another one labeled "Percocet." He eagerly snatched the pill bottles up and tucked them into his shirt.

Mark and Luke were standing at the counter, keeping a close eye out for any approaching zombies. Several creatures milled about through the checkout lines, obliviously unaware of the close human presence. As Scott and Sean returned from the medicine shelves, the two men at the counter motioned for them to stop.

A grossly overweight zombie waddled by, wandering aimlessly toward the shopping carts at front entrance. The four men waited quietly for the big creature to pass before sneaking around the corner back toward the restrooms.

"Let's go," Scott whispered as he ducked back underneath the shadow of the water fountain in front of the women's restroom. Suddenly, a cold hand grabbed him from behind. His head banged loudly into the metal water fountain as he sprung up in surprise, and he fell back against the cinderblock wall.

As the other men rounded the corner through the doorway to the restroom, they spotted a young female zombie with long, blonde hair hovering over Scott. The ghoul crouched down, reaching for Scott's leg on the floor.

Mark smashed his fist into the ghoul's face just as it was about to bite his brother. The beast flew back into the air, crashing violently into the wall. The walking corpse slid down the wall, collapsing on the floor. Then it rolled over and stammered clumsily back to its feet. Its eyes locked onto Mark, and it staggered toward him, swaying awkwardly as it walked. It reached out toward him with its long, polished fingernails just as Sean brought the butt of his rifle down on its head. The powerful blow cracked the creature's skull, and its body crumpled lifelessly to the floor beside Scott.

"You all right, buddy?" Mark asked, reaching a hand out to his brother.

"Yeah," Scott replied as Mark helped him up.

The men rested for a moment, taking drinks from the water fountain as they waited for a chance to move.

"Don't forget about the Sporting Goods," Sean reminded them.

"I need to grab a couple of things while we're over there," Mark said.

"All right," Scott agreed, turning to Luke. "You ready?"

"Go for it."

The four men dashed out across the open floor through a checkout line. They paused for a moment at the candy rack and made their way back through the aisles. As the men rushed through the store, several creatures turned and staggered after them.

Gunfire rang out and one of the ghouls dropped as a steel slug tore into its head.

Luke paused for a moment, breaking the action on his shotgun as he dumped the spent shells out onto the floor. He clicked two more shells into the holes, and snapped the action back into place.

"Let's go!" Mark yelled from a distance.

Luke sprinted off, trailing behind his friends at a steady pace. He darted through the aisles, ending up eventually at the Sporting Goods section and joined the others as they rested against the counter, catching their breath. Leaning over with his hands on his knees, he took several deep breaths through his mouth as his heart pounded rapidly in his chest.

Several zombies faltered slowly toward them in the distance, but they were so far away that the men weren't particularly worried.

Mark browsed through the sports equipment as the others rested at the Sporting Goods checkout counter. He examined several dumbbell sets, testing out the weights in his hands. Luke became preoccupied with a punching bag as he tried on a pair of boxing gloves.

"Let's not forget what we came here for," Sean repeated.

"I gotcha," Scott said. "The girl...gotta find something for the girl." He rummaged through the rack of rifles next to the checkout counter. He spun the rack around slowly, examining the assortment of guns.

"Here we go," Scott announced, pulling a rifle off the rack. "This one's perfect for her." The tag on the rifle read, "Ruger 10/22 Carbine." He grabbed a box of .22 Long Rifle ammunition and stuck it in his pocket.

"You guys ready?" Sean asked.

Luke smacked the punching bag one more time before taking off the gloves and Mark grabbed a weight set as he joined the others at the counter.

"Let's get back to the stockroom," Scott said.

**Nathan Tucker**

The looters gleefully helped themselves to DVD players, flat-screen televisions, cases of beer, clothing, guns, candy and sporting goods. Some simply loaded up shopping carts with all they could hold and boldly pushed them out the doors and down the desolate streets. Some people even carried empty bags, shopping carts and backpacks through the door of the Governor's Square Mall and left with them full of shiny new goods. As they came and went, the looters nodded companionably to one another.

Of course there were many residents who took to theft simply to get food and water from stores bereft of clerks and electricity. But most of the looting was not of that character. While a number of citizens struggled to survive against the hordes of walking corpses that continued to plague the city in increasing numbers, many others seized the opportunity as a free-for-all. As a handful of good-hearted residents strived to help the thousands of injured, those who lacked food and shelter, and the unknown number still trapped in private residences, the psychological blow looters were dealing to the city was overwhelming. The capital of Florida had descended rapidly into a state of anarchy just when organization and cooperation were most essential. The city was now under martial law.

Brent Mathers pulled his patrol car into the deserted parking lot of the Publix shopping center. All of the lights were off in the large 24-hour grocery store, which was normally a bustling center of activity. Scattered shopping carts littered the dimly-lit parking lot in front of the store.

The young, blue-eyed officer let the engine idle, stroking his dark mustache with his thumb as he reviewed the briefings on his laptop again. He still couldn't believe the orders he had received over the radio. All police were now authorized to shoot looters on sight. Although the measures seemed a bit drastic, he understood the reasoning behind the orders. If police officers were authorized to shoot looters, the intelligence would spread quickly among the criminal population. The free-for-all would come to an abrupt end. Only then would the police, fire department, and National Guard be able to do the basics for their suffering compatriots. At least, that's what the authorities hoped would happen.

While sitting quietly in the police cruiser, Brent spotted several ghouls lumbering through the parking lot at a considerable distance. As he watched the bloodthirsty walking corpses wander aimlessly through the lot, he began to wonder why he had even stuck with this job this long. After all, he was a rookie when it began. He had graduated from the academy only a few months prior to the beginning of the chaos that now consumed the city. The thinly-stretched police force was already dwindling less than a week into the disaster. Even many of the seasoned veterans on the force had fallen in the line of duty over the course of the past few days. There wasn't much to look forward to, but he had to stay optimistic. It was all he had left to cling to—the hope and faith that soon things would get better.

But the numbers of the dead had continued to grow exponentially. The death-rate had climbed to alarming figures over the period of only a few days. To add to the number of natural deaths that occurred in the widespread area, the murder-rate quickly skyrocketed to an all-time high as the city fell into chaos. Citizens had begun to turn on each other in a massive upsurge of violence as anarchy reigned. To make matters worse, none of the victims were immune—no matter what the cause of death might be—to the horrible new phenomenon that had suddenly gripped the nation. The corpses of the dead were rising, claiming more and more victims which each new death. It amazed the young officer just how quickly the city had fallen into total disarray.

His reflections quickly subsided as he observed a peculiar site. The distant figures that he had assumed were a group of mindless zombies were now running toward the grocery store. He put the cruiser in drive and moved up for a closer look. As he neared the building, he was able to get a better view of the small gang. It was a group of four young black teenage males, one of whom wielded a metal crowbar in his hand. As soon as the youngsters reached the storefront, the boy with the crowbar struck a large glass window, smashing the glass into pieces. He tossed the crowbar aside and the four hooligans jumped through the opening into the store.

Brent put call out on his radio reporting the incident he had just witnessed as he parked the cruiser in front of the grocery store. As soon as the dispatcher responded and relayed the message to other officers, he jumped out of the patrol car and made his way on foot toward the broken window. When he reached the building, he drew his handgun and shined his flashlight into the store. As he panned the beam of light across the front interior of the dark store, the empty checkout lines came into view. The small group of burglars were nowhere in sight, but he could hear their footsteps as they scurried off into the store aisles. He stepped though the broken window, being careful not to make too much noise as the shards of glass cracked under his shoes.

The interior of the supermarket was enormous. Only a miniscule amount of light was able to penetrate the windows into the spacious building from the street lamps outside. The long, dark aisles that lined the store would have been an easy hiding place for the young hooligans if it had not been for Brent's tremendous running ability. He quickly sprinted between one of the checkout lanes toward the sound of the footsteps just in time to catch sight one of the teenagers. The boy was wearing a white wife-beater shirt and baggy jeans.

"Get your hands up!" Brent cried as he shined his flashlight on the boy's back. The kid glanced back over his shoulder and caught a glimpse of the officer's handgun and he froze, stopping dead in his tracks. The teenager hesitated for a moment and then raised his arms with his back to the young officer.

"Get on the floor," Brent ordered, "face down!" He kept his gun aimed firmly at the young man as he waited for him to comply.

Suddenly, the boy reached into his pants and drew a revolver. Brent fired a shot, hitting the boy in the shoulder. The young man returned fire several times, but his bullets missed the officer by a small margin. The young man quickly disappeared into the aisles as Brent took cover behind a checkout counter.

Brent waited anxiously for a moment on the floor in front of a cash register. Then he peeked over the counter, shining his flashlight down one of the aisles. Seeing that the young man had escaped into the darkness of the store, he put another call out on his radio, signaling to the other officers that shots had been fired.

A few minutes later, Brent heard the sound of police sirens as the cars approached the parking lot. The red and blue flashing lights lit up the front of the store as they parked in front of the windows. Several officers jumped out of the cars and took up positions outside the store with their weapons drawn. From inside the window, Brent waved to the other officers and they advanced into the building.

The sergeant walked straight over to Brent. He was a husky black man in his late forties. He had short, frizzy hair and a thin mustache covering his upper lip, and he carried a pump-action shotgun in one hand.

"Sergeant Harrison," Brent said, waving. "We've got four black males in the building. One of 'em's wounded."

The sergeant nodded and gave orders to the other officers to split up and comb through the aisles one by one. Soon, the front section of the grocery store was lit up by the police flashlights.

Brent made his way down one of the store aisles as two other officers walked behind him to provide cover fire. He emerged from the aisle at the rear of the store near the refrigerated meat section. As he panned his flashlight along the wall, he heard the sound of a creaking door from a narrow hallway next to the meat coolers.

Brent motioned for the other two officers to stay back and cover him as he entered the dark hallway. As he passed in front of a drinking fountain, he noticed some light leaking through the opening along the bottom of the men's restroom door. He leaned his back against the wall and waited for a moment, but heard no sounds from inside. Then he turned and kicked the door open, stiffening his fingers on his handgun as he aimed rigidly into the room.

The fluorescent lights inside the restroom were extremely bright compared to the dark interior of the grocery store. Two urinals protruded from the blue and white checkered tiles on one of the walls, and there were two closed stalls next to the sinks.

The room seemed quiet and empty to the young trooper, but he walked stealthily inside anyway, holding his pistol up as he moved. He walked in front of the first stall, aiming his gun at the door. He quickly kicked it open, but there was only an empty toilet inside. He turned and crept over to the other stall, repeating the process. As the door swung open, an unarmed young man who had been crouching on the toilet seat jumped up and darted out toward the door.

"Don't run out there!" Brent cried. But it was too late. As soon as the boy burst through the door, he was cut down by a barrage of gunfire. Brent tensed up as he watched the bullets pass through the young man's chest. Blood splattered out onto the restroom door as the bullets exited the boy's back and smashed into the wood in a rain of splinters. A wave of nausea suddenly overcame the rookie officer, and he vomited into the restroom sink. He splashed cold water into his face from the faucet, trying to regain his composure.

"You okay in there?" one of the other officers asked from the doorway.

"I'm fine," Brent replied as he held a hand up. He wiped his face with a paper towel and walked out, stepping over the body as he exited.

"Sarge is on the radio calling for backup," the other officer said as Brent took a sip from the drinking fountain. "They've apprehended one of the suspects, but another one's still armed. Can you handle it from here?"

"Yeah, I got it." Brent watched as the other two officers scurried off into the dark store with their weapons drawn. He took another drink of water, and then walked over toward the women's restroom. He kicked the door open, shining his flashlight into the dark room. He scanned the room, but spotted no danger, so he flicked on the light switch. He checked the toilet stalls, but none of them were occupied. Lowering his weapon, he walked back out into the hall.

As he turned the corner, he bumped into someone. Startled, he jumped back away from the figure. It was the young man who had just been shot! Blood poured out from the boy's chest wounds as he took a step toward the young officer. He reached his arms out stiffly and grabbed onto

Brent's wrist. Brent snapped his arm back when he felt the cold, rigid fingers grasp onto him. The sudden realization flashed into the young officer's mind. The boy was dead! He was now a walking corpse.

"Don't come any closer!" Brent cried instinctively as he pointed his handgun at the young man. Although he knew the boy was dead, he hesitated, backing away into the restroom as the door slammed into the boy's face. The rookie officer had never had to shoot anyone in his life. He concentrated for a moment, trying to force the thought that it was only a mindless corpse. Slowly, the door creaked open and the dead boy pushed through. The kid lunged forward with his arms outstretched, and Brent closed his eyes. He squeezed the trigger, and the gun fired a loud shot. Two seconds later, he heard the body collapse onto the linoleum floor with a loud thud, and he opened his eyes. The corpse had fallen on its back, and blood was trickling out from the hole in its forehead.

Several gunshots rang out in the distance, and the young officer hurried out of the restroom into the hallway. As he dashed off into the dimly lit store, he tried to force the gruesome images out of his mind, but they kept replaying in his head. He took a deep breath and shook his head as he approached the other officers in the produce section of the store.

"We got 'em," the sergeant said as Brent walked up. "Dumb bastards tried to put up a fight, but we got 'em."

Brent's gaze fixed on the crumpled bodies that were lying next to a bullet-torn case of apples and oranges. The corpses were surrounded by splattered pieces fruit that had been caught in the crossfire in the apparent shootout. One of the officers had put a carefully-placed bullet into each of the victim's skulls to ensure that the corpses didn't rise again. Blood oozed out onto the floor around the bodies from the holes in their foreheads and other bullet wounds.

Nausea suddenly overwhelmed the young officer again, and he turned his head in disgust, gasping for air.

"Get 'em outta here," the big black man said. Several of the officers covered the bodies with sheets, and one of the men brought a stretcher in from the parking lot. Then the men carried the bodies out of the store.

"No time for investigation?" Brent asked.

"Ain't none left," Sergeant Harrison replied. "And the coroner's overloaded. We gotta clean up after ourselves."

"Should I make a report..."

"Get back to the station," the sergeant cut him off. "Our job here is finished." He turned and walked off.

Brent stood dumbfounded for a moment, staring at the pools of blood that still remained on the floor. The interior of the store became dark again as the squad cars left the parking lot, their headlamps and spotlights no longer lighting up the building.

# 13

The room spun around the big man as he lay uncomfortably across the column of boxes. He stretched his arms out to balance himself, but they flailed around wildly, pummeling the concrete floor below. The stinging lesion on his neck itched, but he couldn't scratch it through the think bandages covering the wound.

"Easy, honey," Samantha said soothingly as she placed her warm hand on the man's chest.

Charlie wrinkled his face in agony, but he calmed down as the comforting hand stroked his skin lightly. He rolled over on his side, grunting as the sharp pains shot through his nerves.

"He needs a doctor," the young woman said, turning to Joe.

"Good luck finding one around here," the blonde-haired man returned. He walked over to the couple and handed a bottle of water to Samantha. She took it and used it to wet a cloth. Dabbing it on the large man's forehead, she looked back over her shoulder.

"What's it like in the city?" she asked.

Joe sat down beside her as he tilted a bottle of beer to his mouth.

"It's a nightmare."

Samantha's eyes widened for a moment, and she looked back down at Charlie.

"Those things are everywhere," Joe continued. "We passed by at least one rescue station that had been knocked out."

"Jesus," Samantha said.

"There's no telling how many people are left—not many, I'd imagine." Joe took a big sip of beer and wiped his mouth on his sleeve.

Samantha sat staring at her injured boyfriend for a moment as the room fell awkwardly silent.

Then a knock came from the double-doors and Joe jumped up, spilling beer on his shirt.

"It's us," a muffled voice leaked through from inside the store. "Let us in."

Joe pushed the barricade of boxes out of the way. He opened the doors and the rowdy group of young men trudged through. Their voices echoed through the stockroom as they entered the room.

"Did you get it?" Samantha impatiently asked.

"Here ya go," Sean said jollily, and tossed a couple of pill jars to the young woman.

She thanked him as she opened the bottle of water and read the label on one of the medicine containers. She placed a tender hand on her boyfriend's cheek, turning his head toward her.

"Here, Charlie," she said. "Can you sit up a little for me, honey?"

The big man groaned and lifted his head as his girlfriend placed a pill in his mouth. She gave him a sip of water, and he swallowed the pill.

Scott emptied his pockets and set the bottles of painkillers on the box next to Charlie, and Samantha examined the containers.

"We got you a little present," Scott said to her as he pulled the rifle strap off his shoulder. He unlocked the safety mechanism from the trigger and handed her the carbine rifle.

"Thanks," she said, rolling her eyes slightly. "Maybe I'll figure out how to work it." She held the gun up to her shoulder and looked down the iron sights. The rifle had no scope, but Samantha didn't mind. She had been to the firing range with Charlie on several occasions and had shot several guns that were very similar to the one she now held. She tested out the action and pulled the trigger. The gun made a clicking noise.

"It's only a twenty-two," Scott said, "but it's semi-automatic and it holds ten rounds. It's the perfect rifle for a smaller person like you because it doesn't have much kick."

Samantha nodded her head, feigning interest with an awkward expression on her face.

"I've heard that if you shoot somebody in the head with a little twenty-two like that," Scott continued, "the bullet doesn't have enough power to exit the skull, so it winds up bouncing around in there, turning the brain into mush."

"Wow," the young woman replied with a hint of sarcasm in her voice. "Thanks for the info."

Scott nodded and tossed the small box of ammunition to Samantha as he walked off to grab a beer.

The young woman picked up the container of Percocet and shook a couple of pills out into her palm. She handed them to Charlie and he swallowed them with another hit from the water bottle. The big man leaned his head back gently as he lay back down on the boxes, and Samantha rested her head beside him. She closed her eyes, dozing off a few minutes later with the rifle still in her lap.

"We'll build a wall across here," Luke said, pointing at the security monitor. His finger traced the outline of the store entrance on the screen. All five of the young friends were gathered together in front of the array of black and white television monitors.

Scott rested his beer on the desk and lit a cigarette. He exhaled the silky smoke into the lingering glow of the monitors, forming a light-blue transparent cloud.

"I know we have all the supplies right there in the hardware department," Sean said. "But what are we gonna use for wood?"

"You know all those tables and desks in the furniture department?" Luke asked.

Sean nodded.

"Those are just the display models," Luke continued. "There's a shitload of those things in boxes that haven't been assembled."

"What about the creatures out there?" Mark asked as he stared at one of the security monitors. "How can we build a wall with those things all over the store?"

"Two people can stand guard while the other three build," Luke replied. "The things move so slow…we'll be able to hold them off easily."

"Let's take a rest first," Sean suggested. "I'm pretty sure we'll need it."

"That's for damn sure," Scott said as he gulped down the rest of his beer.

The five men left the security room and walked back down the hall into the stockroom. As they entered, they noticed that the young couple was still sleeping soundly on the heap of boxes, so they lowered their voices. Three of them sat down quietly against the wall, and Sean laid down on another collection of boxes to take a nap. Scott, however, grabbed another beer from the mini-fridge and walked back down the hallway, disappearing into the security room.

"It'll be easy," Luke whispered. "We'll close off the entrance then we'll kill off the rest of 'em."

Several hours passed, and the young men had all fallen asleep. All of them except for Scott, that is. As he walked through the stockroom toward the little refrigerator, he stumbled over a small box on the floor and fell into a stack of crates. The crates tumbled over, creating a loud ruckus as they crashed to the floor.

Mark was the first to wake. His eyes sprung open, and he rubbed them sleepily. Looking over at the pile of crates that had been knocked over, he spotted his brother, who was picking himself up off the floor.

"Scott?" Mark called out. "You all right, buddy?"

The other men sat up, rubbing the sleep from their eyes.

"I'm fine," Scott answered as he stepped over the crates toward the refrigerator.

"You ready to get started?" Mark asked as he joined his brother at the fridge.

"Hell yeah, man," Scott replied, slurring his speech slightly. "Let's go."

Mark paused, staring at his brother. He watched as Scott flung the refrigerator door open clumsily and snatched another beer off the shelf.

"You're drunk," Mark said, raising his voice.

"I'm fine!" Scott exclaimed as he twisted the cap off the bottle. The metal top fell to the floor, clinking across the concrete as it bounced.

"Look, man," the curly-haired man said as he placed a large hand on his brother's shoulder, "we've got a lot of work to do!"

"I know!"

"You can't go out there like this!"

"I told you, I'm fine!"

Mark turned his back to his brother in frustration. He sighed, looking over to the other men who were rousing from their resting places.

Joe gave Mark an odd look, rolling his eyes to one side as if to say, "I'll take it from here." He walked over to Scott, who was leaning against the wall with one hand.

"You all right, man?" Joe asked.

Scott looked up at him and nodded with a stern expression on his face.

"We're gonna need your help out there," the blonde-haired man said, patting his friend on the shoulder.

"We'd better get moving," Sean advised, looking up at the clock above the double-doors. "It's probably best if we get this done before it gets dark."

"I'll grab a flashlight just in case," Luke said. He walked down the dimly-lit hallway into the security room. He grabbed a long, black flashlight from one of the shelves in the closet. As he walked back through the room on his way out, he noticed an open container on the desk where Scott had been sitting. He stopped for a moment to get a closer look and saw that it was the bottle of OxyContin that Scott had brought back from the pharmacy. It looked like a number of the painkillers were now missing from the container. Luke shook his head and sighed, trying to repress his frustration as he made his way back into the stockroom.

"All right, guys," Luke said to the others. "Get your shit together and let's go." The irritation was evident in his voice. He was disappointed with Scott, but he didn't want to cause a conflict, so he didn't say anything about the half-empty bottle of painkillers he had seen in the security room. But he hoped to God that Scott's intoxicated state didn't pose any serious threats to the difficult task that they were about to undertake.

Samantha woke to the rustling noises that the young men made as they gathered up their weapons.

"Going somewhere?" she asked as she sat up beside Charlie.

"We're going to board up the entrance," Joe replied as he clicked several bullets into his gun's magazine.

"Can I help?" the young woman asked, stroking the new rifle in her lap.

"It's too dangerous," Sean answered as he shook his head.

"I won't get in the way...I promise."

"Maybe next time...your boyfriend needs you here, anyway."

Samantha sighed. She knew they wouldn't let her go with them no matter what she said. *Let the boys have their fun*, she thought.

The young men gathered around the double-doors and started removing the barricade of heavy crates. When they had tossed the last box out of the way, Sean turned to Samantha.

"You're gonna hear some shooting," he said as he cocked the lever on his rifle, "but don't come looking for us. Just make sure you replace the boxes behind the doors after we leave, and you should be safe. I'm assuming you know how to shoot that thing if anything were to happen."

Samantha nodded as she inserted the small ten-round magazine into her rifle.

"And make sure you let us back in when we knock on the doors," Mark added as he pushed one of the shopping carts that they had previously brought back with them through the doors. The men followed him out of the stockroom into the store. The doors closed behind them and Samantha hastily began stacking the boxes back in front the doorway.

The young men rushed through the aisles and headed for the hardware department. They stumbled upon a lone ghoul as they turned a corner, but Luke quickly took care of it with a blast from his shotgun. They continued running and reached the hardware department a few moments later. There were no zombies in sight, but they glanced down the adjacent aisles to be sure. The coast was clear.

"All right guys," Scott said with slurred speech. "Let's get started."

"I'll grab some hammers," Sean offered.

"I'll get the nails," Joe said.

Mark parked the shopping cart in the middle aisle and the men split up, browsing the shelves as they walked their separate ways. When they reconvened a few minutes later,

Luke was standing in front of the checkout counter in the paint section. He had found a hacksaw on one of the shelves. He rested his shotgun on the countertop, letting the barrel hang halfway off the edge. A small shower of sparks emitted from the metal as he sawed the end of barrel off near the stock. The discarded metal plinked across the tile floor as it dropped. Luke held up his newly forged sawed-off shotgun in one hand and swung the break-action hinge across his other wrist. He dumped the spent shells out, replaced them with new ones and snapped the gun back into place.

"Nice!" Mark said, chuckling. "Now let's grab some wood from the furniture department."

The young men dashed off across the store toward the furniture aisle. It was only a short distance from the hardware department, so they arrived quickly at their destination. The furniture shelves were lined with an array of furniture, from office chairs and computer desks to futons and chests of drawers on display. Each display unit had its own respective stack of boxes on the shelf below it. The boxes contained the assembly parts required to put each piece of furniture together. The young men were particularly interested in the wooden furniture, as it contained an assortment of boards of all sizes.

Mark rolled the shopping cart in front of one of the display desks as Luke ripped open one of the boxes. The men pulled some of the boards out and held them up. The wood was polished and sturdy. It would work fine for what they had in mind. They threw the boards into the shopping cart, opening more boxes as they went.

"We'll own this place," Scott boasted as he lit a cigarette. "Those bastards will never know what hit 'em." He sat down on the edge of the aisle and watched as the other men worked.

Soon, the floor was littered with tattered pieces of cardboard from the empty boxes. The young men had managed to fill the shopping cart to the brim with stacks of boards. Mark tossed the last piece of wood on top, and the cart could hold no more.

"We'll probably have to come back for more," Luke said as he patted the stack of supplies. "But this should do for now."

Scott was the first to head toward the front of the store. He eagerly scampered off ahead of the group and rounded the corner aisle. But as soon as he turned the corner, he stopped dead in his tracks. A black zombie with an afro wearing a tan jogging suit lumbered toward him, and Scott took a wild swing at the creature's face. In his intoxicated state, he missed the jab completely and lost his balance. The hungry ghoul tackled him to the floor with an open mouth.

"Scott!" Mark yelled as he let go of the shopping cart and drew his pistol. He stood up straight and took careful aim, but the two bodies were wrestling around wildly on the floor, and he couldn't risk taking a shot for fear that he might accidentally hit his brother. He kept the gun ready, waiting for his chance to take a shot as his brother fought with the ghoul on the tile floor.

The creature rolled on top of Scott, snapping its teeth viciously at him as strings of drool dripped from its mouth into his face. He thrust the palm of his hand against the creature's chin just as it was about to chomp down on his arm and shoved its head back as he struggled to push the heavy beast off of him. As he pressed against its face, the creature bit down onto his fingers. Scott screamed out in agony as the ghoul's rotten teeth broke into the skin just above his fingernails.

Mark walked up and grabbed the back of the zombie's head by its afro. He snapped the creature's neck back, causing its mouth to fly open and Scott pulled his fingers free. Mark held the ghoul's head up with one of his strong arms and placed his Glock up to its temple. He fired a single shot and the creature's brains blew out through the other side of its head. The stream of blood and brain matter spewed out across the floor, staining the white tiles with the gelatinous red substance.

"Thanks," Scott gasped as he pushed the corpse off his body, but his brother only gave him a worried look in return. Scott stumbled to his feet, the effects of the painkillers and alcohol now pulsing strongly through his veins. His heart pumped rapidly in his chest as the rush of adrenaline took hold. A feeling of great exhilaration had consumed him. He was ready for action, whatever might come his way. He felt as if he could take on the world and still stand victorious.

"All right," Scott said, turning to the others with a smirk on his face, "let's get this show on the road!"

Luke shook his head and sighed to himself. Although he was worried about Scott, he was somehow annoyed at the same time by his sheer frivolity.

As the five young men made their way toward the front of the store, they were soon confronted by a large group of ravenous ghouls. The walking corpses loitered around the checkout lanes and entrances, stumbling about aimlessly in droves.

The crackling bursts of fire from semi-automatic and bolt-action rifles echoed across the store as Sean and Joe felled the first few ghouls. The loud sounds of gunfire roused the other creatures, inciting them to focus their entire attention upon the small group of young men. The animated cadavers slowly converged into a large group in front of the men, suddenly stirred up like sharks in a feeding frenzy. They stumbled forward lethargically with their arms outstretched, hungering for the warm, living flesh of the humans.

Scott and Luke stood side by side with their shotguns, blasting away at the front lines of the walking corpses as Sean and Joe continued to fire carefully-aimed sniper-shots. Mark let go of the shopping cart and unstrapped the M-16 from his shoulder. He held the assault rifle at his side, letting loose a barrage of burst-shots into the undead crowd as he walked.

A few minutes later, the last gunshot rang out and a single remaining ghoul fell lifelessly to the linoleum floor, adding to the sea of fallen corpses that now littered the front area of the store. A few zombies still milled about in the nearby aisles, but they had dispersed enough to allow the men to pass.

The brown pickup truck still rested the front of the store surrounded by a sea of shattered glass. More zombies continued to stumble into the store through the compromised doorway in random intervals from the parking lot.

"You guys go on ahead and get started," Sean said, closing one eye as he took aim through the scope on his rifle. "Mark and I will keep you covered." He lined up his crosshairs on a zombie's head that was entering the store and fired a single shot.

Mark rolled the shopping cart beside the pickup truck and left it near the entrance. He jumped in the truck, making sure the keys were still in the ignition, and cranked it. The starter chugged for a moment and then the engine turned over. He quickly threw it in reverse and stepped on the gas pedal. The truck sped out backward into the parking lot as it smashed into a passing creature. The ghoul fell down hard on its back and the tires rolled over it, crushing its skull. He slammed on the brakes a few feet in front of the building and the truck came to a screeching stop. Then he jumped out and ran back inside, bashing the butt of his rifle into the back of another creature's head as he entered the store.

Luke, Joe, and Scott hastily grabbed the hammers and nails from the front of the basket and started constructing the barricade across the entryway as Sean and Mark kept the marauding corpses at bay. Little by little, the wall went up as hungry ghouls attempted to make a feast of the builders. With each fruitless endeavor to grab the young men, the zombies were brought down one by one in a hail of bullets. All the while, the blockade continued to be assembled.

"Charlie?" the young woman asked, suddenly startled by the realization that her boyfriend's eyes were wide-open as they stared vacantly at the ceiling. "Are you awake, honey?"

A sudden trembling enveloped the small woman's body as her fear abruptly took hold. She placed her hand on the big man's forehead. As soon her hand felt the cold skin she immediately snatched it away, her heart jumping inside her. She couldn't believe her eyes.

He was gone. Her one and only... the man she had loved for over three years—she had trouble even forming the words in her mind. Reality suddenly became hazy and distant for the young woman and she struggled to regain her composure. Then the words were abruptly forced into the muddled, emotional pandemonium of her racing thoughts. He was *dead*.

At first, she sat quietly staring in horror and disbelief at the motionless body of the man she had loved for what seemed like an eternity. Then her face suddenly turned red as the inescapable weight of reality fell down upon her. She threw herself upon the body, unable to contain the flood of tears that had now welled up in her eyes. She clung tightly to the big man's lifeless chest, shaking her head uncontrollably in a mixture of sheer disbelief and panic. She stopped for a moment with her ear against his chest and listened for a heartbeat, but all was silent. She cried out his name again and again at the top of her lungs, but nothing she could say or do would ever bring him back—or so she thought.

Unseen by the weeping woman's teary eyes as she poured out her unyielding flood of emotional distress, the large man's fingers suddenly began to twitch at his side.

The large wooden barricade stretched halfway across the entrance when the stack of boards began to dwindle to a small pile in the shopping cart. Several zombies on the other side of the barrier began to push against the half-way completed blockade, but it easily held up against their fragile, rotting bodies.

"We're going to need more wood," Luke announced as he nailed another plank into place.

"I'll run grab some more," Sean offered. "I'll be back in a jiffy." He grabbed another shopping cart from the front and took off into the store.

Another ghoul squeezed in through the edge of the open entrance, and Mark aimed his M-16 at its skull at close range. He pulled the trigger, but the gun only clicked; it was out of ammo. He drew his handgun and fired again, blowing a hole through the creature's skull. He waited for a moment as the lifeless corpse fell backward into the parking lot. There were no more creatures in his immediate site, so he popped the magazine out his assault rifle and started reloading it with shells.

Joe placed the last board from the cart against the wall and Luke hammered one of the edges into place. He pressed the other side against the wooden barricade and Luke repeated the process.

"This is easier than I thought it would be," Scott said as he leaned against the wall and lit a cigarette. "It's like taking candy from a baby." He chuckled loudly, blowing smoke through his nose as he laughed.

Suddenly, an arm reached around the barricade and grabbed Scott's face. It knocked the cigarette out of his mouth as its claws dug into his cheeks. Scott's arms flailed around wildly and he shook his head from side to side as he struggled to break free, but he quickly became dizzy in his intoxicated state. He fell backward against the boards and the ghoul that had grabbed him stumbled around the corner.

"Look out!" Joe cried from the other end of the blockade. He watched in horror as the creature grabbed Scott's injured arm and squeezed the bandage with its claws. Blood oozed out through the edges of the bandage and trickled down his arm as he screamed.

"Jesus Christ!" Mark cried as he dropped his box of ammo and struggled to put the magazine back into his rifle. Shells rolled across the floor as the box hit the tiles.

Luke hastily picked up his sawed-off shotgun and pointed it into the ghoul's face as it buried its fingernails into the wound. He pulled the trigger, firing off a deafening blast as the creature's skull exploded. He shook his wrist after the dispersive discharge from the exceptionally short barrel stung his hand.

"God damn it!" Scott yelled, clutching his wounded arm as he tensed up in agony. His brother rushed to his side to help him up, throwing his arm around his shoulder for support.

"I've got to get him back to the stockroom," Mark said as he slung the M-16 over his shoulder.

"Go on ahead," Luke advised, "we'll finish up here."

Sean emerged from the rear of the store just as Mark walked off with his brother at his side.

"What happened?" Sean inquired as he pushed the shopping cart full of boards up to the entryway.

"He'll be all right," Luke replied. "He just needs to go rest. He shouldn't have been out here to begin with."

Sean didn't quite understand, but he brushed it off and started unloading some of the boards onto the floor. He handed a board to Joe and the two cousins continued with the construction of the barricade.

When Mark and Scott reached the entrance to the stockroom, Mark knocked loudly on the double-doors. He waited several moments, but there was no reply. He struggled with the weight on his shoulder as his brother leaned against him and he knocked again.

Suddenly, he heard a high-pitched scream from behind the doors. He eased his brother down onto the floor and helped him lean against the wall. Then he walked a few steps away from the entrance and charged against the double-doors, slamming into them shoulder-first with all his might. The boxes on the other side of the door flew back and the doors swung open. Mark crashed through the doorway and stumbled forward onto the concrete floor, bracing his fall with his hands.

As soon as he looked up, he caught sight of Samantha, who had fallen into a stack of boxes in a corner of the room. Her boyfriend was hovering over her with his massive arms outstretched toward her face. She was kicking and screaming as the huge man towered above her. Blood trickled down his chest from the wound on his neck.

"Step away from her!" Mark cried as he cocked the lever on his rifle. As took aim with the rifle, he noticed the unnatural bluish color of the burley man's skin.

"No, Charlie!" Samantha cried as the big man opened his jaws to bite her. Just before the big man's teeth clamped down on her arm, a bullet penetrated the back of his head from the M-16, tearing through his brain as it exited his forehead. Blood squirted out from the hole into Samantha's face as the big man's lifeless body fell limply to the concrete floor.

"No!" the young woman screamed as she fell on top of her boyfriend's motionless body. Tears streamed down her cheeks as she embraced the body, squeezing it firmly with her tiny arms as she rocked back and forth. She pressed her face into the fallen man's back, weeping uncontrollably.

Mark stood silently observing the tragedy before him as a wisp of smoke rose from the barrel of his gun. He wasn't sure whether to hug the young woman consolingly or back away and let her cry. He stood rigid, unable to speak or move for a few moments. Then he was suddenly overwhelmed with pity for the young woman and he rushed to her side, holding her tightly as she wept upon his shoulder.

**Nathan Tucker**

The young woman had cried all night long. Mark stayed up with her, listening to her and consoling her throughout the night while the others slept. They had put Charlie's body in the walk-in dairy cooler at the rear of the store before going to bed.

The six survivors were now safely barricaded inside the massive store. Their only cause for concern was the fairly large number of zombies that were now trapped inside the store. The large stack of crates had to remain in place at the double-doors to keep the creatures out of the stockroom.

The morning sun peaked over the horizon outside the large superstore, casting its orange glow upon the ghouls that wandered about in the vast parking lot. The creatures were still crowded around outside the entrances, but were now unable to get inside.

Mark and Samantha were still awake from the night before, sitting on a stack of boxes as Mark spoke soft words of consolation. Samantha's crying had subsided—at least for the moment. The other young men slowly began to rouse from their sleep as the morning dragged on. Scott, however, still slept soundly.

Mark grabbed several frozen dinners from the mini-refrigerator and put them in the microwave. He handed Samantha a bottle of water and opened one for himself. He sat back down beside her and patted her softly on the shoulder with his massive hand as she drank.

In some ways, the big, curly-haired man reminded Samantha of Charlie. She took comfort in his muscular arms, but nothing could ever replace the man she had loved. She already missed him so much, but it still hadn't totally sunk in yet that he was truly gone. She kept waiting for him to emerge from around a corner at any moment.

"Morning," Joe greeted as he sat up, rubbing his eyes.

"Hey," Mark said with a solemn look on his face. Although he hadn't slept, he wasn't tired.

"You been up all night?" Joe asked as he stood up and walked toward the employee restroom.

"Yeah," Mark replied. The timer went off on the microwave and he got up. He handed one of the meals to Samantha and she quietly accepted it. The two sat together in somber silence as they ate.

Sean sat down across from them and peeled a banana. He gave Samantha a consoling look, unsure of what to say to her. He felt deeply sorry for her loss, but he just wasn't good with words. An awkward silence fell upon the room as they sat eating their breakfast.

A few minutes later, Luke walked up, and the tension eased.

"Hey guys," he greeted them. "Good job last night. We got it all closed off."

Sean and Mark nodded, but Samantha neglected to respond as she sat quietly eating—her mind was elsewhere.

"If we can take care of the rest of those creatures," Luke continued, "this place will be ours."

"How many of those things you reckon are still inside?" Mark asked.

"Not sure," Luke replied. "It shouldn't be that difficult, though."

"It'll be a massacre," Joe cut in as he emerged from the restroom. He had overheard his cousin from inside the small room.

The uproar of voices had woken Scott from his slumber. He sat up on one of the boxes. His head was spinning from the night before. With each sound came a shooting pain through his head, and his mouth was as dry as sand. He got up and grabbed a bottle of wine from the stack of goods next to the little refrigerator.

"Good morning, Scott," Mark greeted his brother. "A little early for that, isn't it?"

"Gotta chase the hangover," Scott replied coldly with a disgruntled look on his face. He tilted the bottle up and took a big swig of the wine. Luke gave him a stern look as he drank.

"We'll need to pick up some more bullets from the Sporting Goods before we start," Sean said. "I'm running low on ammo."

"What are you guys planning now?" Scott asked as he held the wine bottle at his side.

"We're gonna kill off the rest of the zombies in the store," Mark replied.

"Great," Scott returned as he took another sip of wine. "When do we start?"

The room fell awkwardly silent for a moment as no one responded. Then, Mark stood up and put a hand on his brother's shoulder.

"Maybe you should sit this one out, buddy," he suggested.

A disheartened look suddenly crossed Scott's face. He quickly gulped down another sip of wine from the bottle.

"I mean," Mark said, grasping for the words as he realized how his words might have sounded, "maybe you should give that arm a rest."

"My arm's fine," Scott retorted, wrinkling his brow in a stern expression as he spoke. He rubbed the bandages softly with the wine bottle in his other hand.

"I'm going with you," Samantha suddenly spoke up. She hadn't spoken a word in hours, but she perked up all of a sudden, looking much more alert than before. She grabbed her .22 rifle and stood up beside Mark.

Scott rolled his eyes with his back turned to the young woman, and took another hit from the wine bottle.

"All right," Mark agreed, turning to the young woman. "Just stick with me and you'll be all right."

"When are we going?" Scott asked impatiently. "I'm ready now."

"Why don't we trade guns?" Sean offered, looking over at Scott. "You'll be able to stay back a good distance with my rifle…since you're injured and all."

Scott thought about it for a moment, almost losing his cool. He was about to start yelling when Sean smiled at him. He turned his head away, pausing for a few awkward moments of silence. He felt the wine taking effect as he stood there, and a calming sensation pulsed through his body. Finally, he nodded his head in agreement and tossed his shotgun to Sean.

"Cool," Sean said with a smile. "Here ya go…just be careful. It's got a hairpin trigger, and it'll kick you good if you're not ready for it."

"Gotcha," Scott replied as he took the rifle from Sean's hands.

"Let's just take it easy on this," Mark said as he gently pulled the wine bottle from Scott's hand.

Scott nodded. He took one last guzzle of wine, and let his brother take the bottle.

"Is everybody ready?" Luke asked.

The others nodded, including Joe who was sitting quietly on a box finishing off a can of sardines.

"All right, then…let's go!"

The group moved the boxes from the double-doors and rushed out into the store. Several creatures had assembled outside the entrance to the stockroom, but Sean and Luke took them out quickly with a couple of shotgun blasts. Then the group headed over to the Sporting Goods.

"What caliber is this thing?" Scott asked as he reached the ammo counter.

"Here ya go," Sean responded as he tossed a box of .30-30 rounds from the glass case. The others grabbed more ammunition as well, filling their pockets with various bullets and shotgun shells.

Joe noticed that Sean seemed to be fairly knowledgeable about guns. He looked down for a moment, examining his Scout rifle, and then looked back over at the auburn-haired man.

"Sean," he said, "can you help me find something with a little more power?"

Sean turned around with a smile on his face.

"Sure," he replied. He walked over to the revolving rifle rack and spun the wheel around. "How about a thirty ought six?"

"Is that the most powerful thing they got?"

Sean paused, spinning the rack again. His eyes fixed on a Remington Model 700 with a walnut stock. He picked it up and examined the bolt-action on the weapon.

"Here's what you're looking for," Sean said as he handed the large rifle to the blonde-haired man and tossed him a box of .300 Weatherby Magnum rounds.

"Thanks," Joe said as Scott handed him the keys. He unlocked the safety lock from the trigger and loaded the gun.

A lone zombie suddenly stumbled around the corner of a nearby aisle, but a loud gunshot rang out from above, and the creature dropped. Sean and Joe looked up to see Scott, who had climbed up a deer stand that was on display.

"I see you found a good spot," Joe said as he clicked the bolt on his rifle into place.

"Yup," Scott replied. He lit a cigarette and looked through the rifle scope again as the cigarette dangled from his lips. He fired off another shot over the top of the shelves at another creature in the distance.

Joe climbed up on the tall shelf next to an aisle full of bicycles. He sat on the ledge and looked through the scope on his new rifle. He lined the crosshairs up on a ghoul that had crossed out into the middle walkway aisle. He applied pressure to the trigger and fired a deafening blast from the gun. The kick on his shoulder from the force of the powerful blast nearly caused him to tumble backward off the ledge, but he caught himself with one hand.

"Nice," Joe said with a smile. He was greatly pleased with the supremacy of his new weapon. "I'll stay back with Scott and we'll pick 'em off from here."

"Sounds good," Mark said as walked up to the ammo counter. He turned to Samantha, who was staring silently across the store at a small group of zombies in the distance. "Stay close to me, and if you run out of ammo I'll cover you while you reload."

The young woman nodded.

"All right," Luke said as he joined them at the counter. "Let's go!"

Sean, Mark, Samantha, and Joe charged down the middle aisle. An eruption of gunfire broke out at they closed in upon the crowd of ghouls. Scott and Luke felled the walking corpses one by one with carefully-aimed shots from their sniper positions. Rapid, cracking bursts of gunfire echoed down the aisles from Samantha's semi-automatic carbine rifle.

Soon, the heavily-armed group of young people had combed through every aisle in the store, mowing down ghouls as they marched. The white tiles on the floor became drenched in blood, and a multitude of dead bodies now littered the store. As the band of young zombie-hunters reconvened at the Sporting Goods, Joe fired off another thunderous shot from his high-powered rifle, and the last-remaining creature's head burst into an explosion of blood and brain matter.

"There's gonna be a lot of rotting corpses stinking up the place," Scott said from the top of the deer stand as the others returned from their hunt. He put an unlit cigarette in his mouth and climbed down the ladder.

"We'll have to clean up," Luke said as he rested his sawed-off shotgun on the counter.

"What should we do with the bodies?" Scott said as he leaned his rifle against the counter and lit the cigarette.

"We could dump them off the loading docks in the stockroom," Joe suggested as he jumped down from the bicycle shelf.

"No way, man," Mark cut in. "Those roll-down doors are hard to mess with. Those creatures would overrun the place in no time if we tried to keep them open."

"What about the dairy cooler?" Samantha asked.

"Too small," Scott replied. "They wouldn't all fit."

"There're a lot of freezers in the frozen-food section," Mark said.

"That would ruin the food," Joe replied. "We're going to need all the food we can get. Who knows how long we'll be in here?"

"There's a big open area behind the checkout lanes," Luke said. "We could burn the bodies there."

"That would set off the sprinkler system and the smoke alarms," Sean surmised. "Those alarms might even have a connection to the Fire Department or another agency. We don't need that kind of attention."

"What about the Garden Center?" Joe asked as his eyes lit up with an idea. "It's open-air out there and enclosed by that tall metal fence."

"But our cars are out there," Mark said.

"We could easily move them against the fence," Joe replied.

"Joe's right," Scott agreed. "We'll just have to push some of the plants and stuff out of the way, but there should be enough room out there."

"All right," Luke said. "Let's grab some of those four-wheeled dollies from the stockroom."

"I probably wouldn't be of much help lifting those heavy things," Samantha said. "I'll get mop and bucket and try to clean up some of the mess."

The young men agreed, and they walked off to the stockroom while the young woman headed over to the cleaning products aisle. She picked out a large mop and some other cleaning supplies and filled a bucket with water from the sink in the stockroom. She started mopping up some of the blood and gore from the store floor while the young men rounded up the corpses on dollies, stacking them in a large pile outside in the Garden Center.

Scott moved his car back to make room for the heap of corpses.

"I just thought of something," Sean said. "I don't know how long we're gonna be here. But if we have to leave in a hurry, it might not be a bad idea to have one of the cars parked around back."

"The loading docks?" Scott asked.

"Yeah," the red-haired man replied. "Might make for a quick escape—if we were to need one."

"Sounds good," Scott said. "I'll cover you if you want to move the van."

"All right," Sean said, and he got in the driver's seat of the van.

"Keep 'em distracted while we're gone," Scott said to Luke as he pointed at the crowd of walking corpses. "But don't let 'em in." He got in the backseat of the van and stood up through the sunroof.

"Be careful," Luke said, and he untied the water hose from the gate. He swung the gate open and the van took off into the parking lot. Then he closed it quickly before the zombies could get in.

Sean drove around behind the large store to the loading docks. There were a few random ghouls roaming around in the back lot, but most of them had moved around front toward the Garden Center. Sean backed up onto one of the loading ramps in front of a roll-down door, and pulled the parking brake.

Scott fired a loud shotgun blast from the sunroof of the van at an approaching ghoul. The creature's head burst open as the buckshot smashed into its skull, and its body crumpled to the pavement. Then the two men jumped out and ran around the corner toward the Garden Center.

"Come on!" Joe yelled through the bars of the tall fence. "Hurry up, guys!"

Scott smashed the butt of his shotgun into a zombie's face as he rounded the corner. He cocked the pump, ejecting an empty shell, and blew a hole into another creature's head with a single blast.

"Open the gate!" Sean yelled, and he smashed his fist into a ghoul's jaw as the two young men approached the front lot.

Luke swung the metal gate open just in time as the men rushed through, and he struggled to get it closed again against the weight of the marauding gang of corpses. Scott and Sean helped him push it closed, but one of the creatures fell through the opening, blocking the gate from closing all the way.

"Pull it through!" Scott yelled as he leaned against the metal bars.

Sean grabbed the zombie's wrists and dragged it inside as Scott and Luke tried to push the gate closed. But too many zombies were now pressing against it, and the men struggled against the massive pressure. Just as they were about to give out, Mark rushed up and slammed all two-hundred and forty-three pounds of his weight against the gate, and it slammed shut. While the Walker brothers held it in place, Luke tied the water hose around the bars, locking it into place.

Mark let go of the bars and walked over to the zombie that Sean had dragged across the concrete. He drew his Glock and fired a quick shot into the creature's skull.

The young men breathed a sigh of relief, and took a short rest. Then they continued on with their cleaning work.

After a couple of hours, the men had cleared the store of the fallen corpses. While Sean and Scott moved their vehicles away from the pile, Joe and Mark made a clearing around it by pushing plants and other flammable objects out of the way. Luke got several bottles of lighter fluid from the charcoal and grilling shelf in the store. When he returned, he doused the pile of bodies in the fluid until it was completely soaked. Then Scott flicked a cigarette butt into the pile and it lit up instantly into a huge flaming mass of dead bodies.

The zombies that were crowded around the metal fence backed away into the parking lot when the flames went up. They shielded their eyes from the flames as they spread out.

"They don't seem to like fire," Mark said as he gazed out at them between the bars in the gate.

"Dumb bastards," Scott snarled as he lit another cigarette.

They stood around for a few more minutes gazing at the massive bonfire as it consumed the enormous heap of corpses. Then they went back inside the store and helped Samantha clean the floor.

"It'll be nice to finally sleep on something other than a stack of boxes," Sean said as he rolled a mop bucket toward the stockroom.

"Yeah," Joe agreed. "I saw some comfortable-looking futons on the furniture aisle."

"I'm so glad we found this place after all," Mark said as he dipped his mop into the bucket.

"I know," Luke said with wide eyes and a huge grin on his face. "It's perfect."

"Perfect…" Samantha mumbled to herself, inaudible to the others, as she stared blankly at the tiles on the floor.

## 15

The Tallahassee Police Department building was a scene of utter chaos. The remaining officers of the thinly-stretched police force marched in and out of the main entrance, escorting detainees that had been caught looting or partaking in other crimes in the havoc-stricken city. Secretarial workers and other office employees rushed about frantically through the halls and offices, running into each other and knocking over the various furnishings as they moved. The normally calm corridors of the station were now filled with the buzzing of loud voices and rhythmic footsteps.

Telephone and data transmission services were still down. All emergency repair crews that had been dispatched to fix the communication lines were missing—and had probably fallen victim to the hordes of walking corpses that had increased at an unbelievable rate over the past several days. There was no longer any method of communication between state and federal authorities—or even between the local police precincts, for that matter. The city had rapidly descended into a complete state of turmoil.

Brent Mathers pushed his way though the bustling hallway. The marble floor was littered with discarded report papers, soda cans, and Styrofoam cups. He walked into the break room and poured a cup of coffee. He sat down at the rectangular table in the center of the room, and flipped through a newspaper, which was dated more than a week ago. The headline on the front of the paper read, *THE DEAD WALK*. As Brent sipped on his coffee, a gray-haired officer with huge glasses poked his head through the doorway.

"Sarge's callin' everybody to the meetin' room," the older officer said in a thick, Southern accent.

"All right," Brent replied, looking up from his newspaper. He recognized the older officer as Walter Sherman, a man in his late fifties who had probably been on the force longer than the young officer had been alive. Brent took another leisurely sip of the hot liquid and leaned back in his chair, stroking his mustache thoughtfully.

"Better get a move on it," the gray-haired man added. "He don't sound too happy."

Brent sighed and followed Walter down the hall. The droning sound of voices grew louder as the men approached the meeting room at the end of the corridor. Inside the room, only half the seats were filled. The small group of officers sat facing the front of the room, drinking coffee and conversing rowdily. Their faces were covered in sweat and their uniforms were disheveled, as if they hadn't showered in days.

"All right, gentlemen," Sergeant Harrison called out from the front of the room in a loud, booming voice. "Let's quiet down now."

Brent and the older officer sat down at the back of the room.

"As you all know," the big black man said, "looters are to be shot on sight. Unarmed civilians found walking the streets are to be taken into custody and delivered to the rescue stations. You've all done an excellent job this past week."

"Yeah," Brent whispered to the older officer beside him. "When do we get paid?"

"We've got a lot on our hands," the sergeant continued. "And you men are all we've got left. But we're still left with the difficult task of enforcing martial law."

A small uproar of voices filled the room as the officers began to protest.

The sergeant raised his voice and said, "Now, listen here!" His booming voice caught the attention of the small crowd and a hush fell over the room. "With help from the National Guard we can deal with this situation properly. I've received new orders from the governor, himself!"

The buzzing of voices filled the room once again, but this time it wasn't in protest.

"Listen up," the sergeant continued his spill. "Now I know you guys are gettin' edgy. I gotta admit…I am too. But just hear me out."

The chatter continued for a moment, but slowly died out as the sergeant paused intentionally.

The big black man took a deep breath and continued, "The governor has authorized state and city police to seize supplies from overrun businesses and commercial enterprises as we see fit!"

Another outburst of voices echoed through the meeting hall, but a lot of the officers leaned forward out of curiosity.

"We're stretched thin and we're runnin' out of resources fast," Sergeant Harrison said. "Now's our chance to reclaim some of our losses."

The room grew silent, and the big black man took another deep breath.

"There ain't much left that hasn't been hit by looters," he continued. "But that's part of your new assignment."

"Another one?" a voice said from the back row. Another burst of chatter filled the room, and some of the men chuckled to one another.

"You've all been assigned to a special unit," the sergeant said, and the room grew quiet again. "We're going out toward Monticello. There are still some businesses out there that haven't been knocked over yet. And we're going to see to it that they stay that way. You men will be able to take what you need as you see fit. Report to my office in the morning—oh-eight-hundred hours. And don't make me come lookin' for ya." With that, the big black man turned and walked out of the room.

The room became filled with chatter again, and several officers walked out into the hall. Brent sat back in his chair. He couldn't believe what he had gotten himself into. If only he had listened to his girlfriend, he might still be at home with her, able to protect her and comfort her. She had asked him not to go back to work when the outbreak first started, but he didn't listen to her. He had felt it was still his duty to serve the public. But little did he know the absolute chaos that was about to break out. And here he was at the police station, getting ready to go out and shoot unarmed civilians. As strange and ironic as it seemed, he found that deep within him, he had the notion that it was the only thing that would keep him sane now. He needed a sense of duty—something to keep him going in this world gone mad. Not to mention the shelter and safety that the police force provided for him.

"Lights out," a voice said from the hallway.

Brent shook his head, startled from his thoughts. He looked around, noticing that he was the only one remaining in the room.

"You coming," the voice asked, "or you gonna just sit there like a log?"

"I'm coming," Brent replied. He stood up, pausing for a moment at his seat as he saw that the voice belonged to Walter. Then he put on his jacket and followed the other officer, who turned off the lights and closed the door. The two men walked into the lobby to the front desk.

"I guess we're ready to turn in," Walter said to the overweight woman sitting behind the desk.

"Okay," the woman replied. She pressed a button on the wall beside her, and a buzzer sounded on the electronic lock of the door next to the two officers. The door swung open slowly, and the two men entered into the corridor leading to the jail cells. The police department had rounded up a lot of their prisoners and made many of them share the same cells to make room for the members of the department to use a section of the jail for sleeping quarters. The department used one whole block of cells, in which they had assigned shifts for the officers to take turns sleeping. Brent had been assigned to the 2:00 AM shift. It was now 1:48 AM, so the officers from the previous shift would be getting up very soon.

As the two men walked toward their cells, Brent thought about the prisoners in the other cell blocks. He was sure there were two many prisoners for the department to be able to use a whole block of cells, even though they had forced the prisoners to share more cells. He wondered if they had released some of the minor offenders to make room. Or even worse...but he didn't want to think about that. Releasing them into the outside world was bad enough. Where would the prisoners go? Ironically, jail or prison was probably one of the safest places to be, these days.

Brent had heard a lot of horror stories about things that had gone on in rescue stations, and was glad that he had a relatively safer place to live for the time being. However, his girlfriend was probably at one of those rescue stations, and he worried for her safety. Although he and his girlfriend had only been together for a few months before the outbreak had started, he still cared deeply for her. It hurt him to let her go, but he felt it was best for the both of them at the time, when the outbreak first began. Although she argued strongly against his decision, he chose to serve the public instead of his own selfish interests—at least that is the way he wanted to see it. His girlfriend went to her parents' house, even though martial law had been declared, and all of the citizens had been instructed to move to centrally designated areas of the city. Brent hadn't heard from them since that day, because telephone and other communication services had been mysteriously inoperable since the first day of the outbreak.

The two officers entered a jail cell as two others who had been sleeping gathered their belongings and left.

"You want the top or the bottom bunk?" the gray-haired officer asked, setting his bag down in the corner of the concrete cell.

"I don't care," Brent replied.

"In that case, I'll take the bottom. Gettin' hard for these ol' legs to do any climbin', these days."

"I hear you," Brent said, pulling himself up to the top bunk. He breathed a long sigh as he leaned back against the pillow. It had been a long day, and he knew he would need as much rest as he could get. There were only four hours left until he was supposed to report back to the sergeant's office. The lights went out, and he closed his eyes, trying to quell his racing thoughts so that he could get some much-needed sleep.

"Ain't it a shame?" Walter's voice came suddenly from below.

Brent opened his eyes, somewhat startled by the sudden sound. "What?"

"We're out here riskin' our asses to save people, and we gotta sleep in these damn jail cells like a buncha criminals. And we ain't even gettin' paid for it."

"Technically, we're supposed to get paid…" Brent stared blankly at the concrete ceiling as he listened to the older Southern man ramble on.

"Bullshit. You really think we'll see a dime from them bastards? Hell, most of 'em are probably dead now…or holed up in some top-secret bunker somewhere."

"You're probably right," Brent said softly. He rolled over on his side, closing his eyes again.

"We'd be better off on our on," Walter added.

Brent didn't respond, but the words repeated in his head as he drifted off to sleep.

"You gonna sleep all day?" the words suddenly shook Brent from his deep sleep.

The young officer rolled over, face down on his pillow. He hadn't had any dreams, at least none that he could remember. It seemed like as soon as he had closed his eyes, Walter had awoken him.

"What the hell time is it?" Brent asked, rubbing the sleep from his eyes.

"Six A.M."

"Shit!" Brent sat up quickly in the top bunk, bumping his head on the ceiling.

"Yeah," Walter said with a hint of sarcasm in his tone. "Harrison's gonna piss his pants if we don't get our asses down to his office right now."

Brent didn't even bother combing his matted hair before he left. He followed the older officer out of the cell down the hallway and into the lobby.

"Morning," the hefty woman at the front desk greeted as the two officers. She opened her mouth to engage the men in friendly conversation, but they kept walking, only nodding at her as they passed by her desk in a hurry.

As the two officers neared the sergeant's office, they could hear him yelling from down the hall.

"You go tell 'em to get their asses down here immediately," Harrison said. "They got five minutes, or their asses are toast! Now go!"

"No need," Brent said as he and Walter entered the room. "We're already here." He and the older officer took a seat in the corner of the room.

"What the hell took you so long?"

Brent looked at his watch. It was only four minutes after six. He shrugged and said, "Sorry."

The big black man sighed and walked to his desk. He picked up a metal folding chair, slammed it down to the floor, and sat down on it. He paused for a few moments, gazing at the men in front of him. They had all served the police force well during the last week, which was why they had been selected for this special unit. Although Harrison wasn't very fond of the task ahead of them, the order had been handed down to him from higher officials. He knew that the job wouldn't be easy, but someone had to do it, and the men that now stood in his office were the best men for the job.

As the sergeant surveyed the men, a soft chatter had enveloped the room as the officers spoke quietly among themselves, their voices and random coughs echoing off the walls.

"All right," Sergeant Harrison said, holding up his hand to signal the men to quiet down. "Now I know you've all been trained to deal with common criminals. You've all taken out drug dealers, thieves, and violent offenders. But today we have two enemies. Not only are we going to deal with the looters and anarchists ravaging the city, but we're also going to have to fight the walking dead. None of you, including myself, have received any training for the task we're about to undertake. But I know each and every one of you has what it takes to get the job done. It ain't gonna be easy, but I know you can do it. Not only do you have a duty to this community—you have a duty to this country. We're all counting on you. Now let's go out there and show 'em who's boss."

Sergeant Harrison led the men out of his office down the hallway. The woman at the front desk unlocked a large metal door on the opposite side of the lobby, and the men walked through into an enclosed garage filled with squad cars and several S.W.A.T. vans. The sergeant walked to one of the walls and unlocked a large metal locker. He swung the door open, revealing a vast assortment of assault rifles, submachine guns, ammunition, smoke grenades, and other tactical equipment.

"Help yourselves," Harrison said, opening another locker that stood several feet from the first one. In the next locker, a collection of specially designed jumpsuits hung from a rack. Above the jumpsuits, bulletproof vests and bandoliers hung from the top rack.

Without hesitation, the team of officers grabbed various weapons, ammunition, and tactical gear, and suited up in the S.W.A.T. regalia. Harrison surveyed his men, allowing a slight smile to cross his hardened face. He was pleased with the demeanor his men exhibited. He had great confidence that they had what it took to complete their mission.

"All right," Harrison said with a tinge of excitement in his voice. "Let's get this show on the road."

The men loaded the heavier weapons into the vans, which already contained some extra weapons and ammunition. Some of the men broke up into pairs and got into police cruisers. The others loaded up into the vans, which had benches on each side of the rear cab.

"Mathers," the sergeant said, sticking his head out of the window of his police cruiser. "You're with me."

The young officer sat in the van in deep thought, oblivious to the sergeant's orders.

"Mathers!" Harrison repeated, waving his hand around. "Let's go!"

Brent realized the sergeant was talking to him, and jumped out of the van. He sat in the passenger seat of Sergeant Harrison's squad car.

Harrison pressed a button on a remote control, and the large metal door at the far end of the garage lifted up slowly. He drove right up to the door, waiting for it to open enough to drive through. The other vehicles engines cranked in unison and the concrete walls of the garage reverberated with the sound of revving motors. The officers turned on their headlights, as it was still dark in the early morning hours.

As soon as the metal door had risen several feet, a small gathering of zombies moved into the garage toward the vehicles. The officers in the cars near the front of the garage, including Brent, fired their handguns from of the windows of the cruisers. One by one, the creatures dropped until there were none of them left standing. Harrison stomped on the gas, crushing the fallen ghouls' bones beneath the wheels of his cruiser as it sped out into the city streets. He hit the button on the remote control again as soon as the other vehicles were outside the garage, and the door came back down just in time to stop another swarm of creatures from entering.

The visibility was low in the darkness of the early morning, and a light rain fell on the city streets, illuminated by the vehicles' headlights. Steam rose from the evaporating water on the concrete, creating an eerie scene as walking corpses wandered aimlessly through the streets. Harrison swerved back and forth on the road to avoid wandering ghouls, but the large vans behind him plowed right through the creatures.

An uneasy feeling took hold of Brent as the enormity of the situation became evident to him. His palms began to sweat and his legs trembled in the passenger seat of the cruiser. Hideous faces of the undead flashed before his eyes as the headlights shined on the creatures they passed. The constant rhythm of the windshield wipers tapping back and forth on the glass, squeaking as they pushed the water from the light rain, seemed to grow louder with each passing second. The young officer shifted nervously in his seat, trying to catch his breath and regain his composure.

"You all right over there?" Harrison asked, glancing over at his passenger.

"Yeah," Brent replied, trying his hardest to sound at ease. "I'm fine." In reality, his thoughts were racing faster than the sergeant's squad car.

"There ain't nothing to worry about with me at the wheel." The sergeant swerved quickly to avoid another small group of ghouls.

Brent reached into his pocket and produced a small medicine bottle. He quickly popped it open in his trembling hands, and swallowed two of the pills. Several minutes later, his nerves began to calm down, and the shaking went away. As the young officer sat back in his seat, the sounds around him became clearer and more distinct as his body relaxed. He gradually became more aware of his surroundings, and he gazed out of the passenger window. The rain had slowed to a light sprinkle, and the orange morning sunlight had peaked over the horizon.

As the vehicles approached the outskirts of town, the sheer numbers of the creatures diminished. There were still zombies lingering in the streets, but they more spread out here than in the inner city.

The two men rode in silence for several minutes, each of them quietly scanning their surroundings as the other vehicles followed closely behind. Then, after a brief period, Sergeant Harrison broke the silence.

"Our first location of interest should be coming up on the other side of this hill," Harrison said, looking at a map he had spread out across the steering wheel.

Brent nodded. The nervousness suddenly took hold of him again at the sergeant's words.

"Radio the others," the sergeant ordered. "This is it up here."

The young officer obeyed, picking up the radio piece. He relayed the message into the microphone, and an affirmation came in response over the speakers.

As the squad car passed over the top of the hill, a large sign came into view. It read, "Wal-Mart Supercenter."

Brent sat up in his seat, staring in revulsion at the large mob of zombies that wandered about aimlessly in the vast parking lot.

"Perfect," the sergeant said, steering left and right to avoid random ghouls as the convoy of police vehicles drove through the lot toward the large building. "Looks like we've found us a winner."

The young officer looked in the direction that the big man was pointing and spotted a silver-colored car parked safely behind the Garden Center fence.

**Nathan Tucker**

The small band of survivors roamed about happily inside the superstore, barricaded in safety from the horrors that were going on outside in the world around them. Several days had passed since they had eradicated the ghouls from inside the store. They ambled through various sections of the building, enjoying the endless entertainment of the bountiful supply of toys and other goods that the large retail outlet had to offer. Mark and Joe ventured over to the electronics department and played video games on the various consoles that they had hooked up to a vast array of widescreen televisions. Luke browsed through paperback novels on the bestseller rack of the magazine aisle. Sean discovered a wide selection of gourmet coffees from around the world, and he collected them into a shopping basket to try out later. Samantha distracted herself in the beauty department, trying on makeup and hair products in front of the vanity mirrors.

The survivors were all enjoying the luxuries of the huge commercial center—all of them except for Scott, that is. The pain in his arm had become excruciatingly unbearable. As he tossed and turned on one of the black futons that the young men had assembled in the stockroom, the room began to spin wildly around him. He cried out with a loud voice, but no one was there to hear him. He jerked to one side as a sharp pain jolted him, and his body crashed down onto the concrete floor. His vision became blurry as he scanned the room from the floor. He crawled dizzily over to an empty box and grabbed the open bottle of Percocet that rested on top. Then he dumped several pills out into his mouth and swallowed them. The agony was almost unbearable now, and he collapsed onto his side. He rocked back and forth on the floor, waiting feverishly for the painkillers to take effect.

Unknown to the survivors inside the store, the parking lot was now host to movement other than the walking dead. Several tactical vans had arrived in front of the building, along with a small escort of squad cars. Troopers dressed in full S.W.A.T. regalia, armed with automatic rifles and submachine guns, rushed out of the parked vans and took up positions outside the store. Several shots rang out as some of the men fired into the small crowd of zombies that were gathered in front of the entrances.

"What the hell was that?" Mark exclaimed, dropping the video game controller in surprise.

"What the hell was *what*?" Joe said.

Mark paused for a moment and raised his hand to his ear, listening intently to his surroundings. The soft background music still played over the store speakers. Then the muffled sound of gunfire became audible in the distance.

"That!" Mark cried.

Joe stood up and turned off the television in front of him.

A moment later, Sean came running into the electronics department. "Did you guys hear that?"

"Yeah," Mark said. "Sounds like gunfire!"

"Somebody's out there!" Joe yelled.

"Where are the others?" Sean asked frantically.

"Not sure," Mark replied. "Let's find 'em, though. I think I know where Samantha is."

"I'll grab some weapons from the stockroom," Joe said.

"Good idea," Sean said. "I'll look for Luke."

The magazine aisle was very close to the checkout lanes in the front of the store. Luke had heard the gunshots very clearly from his position. When the shots rang out, it startled him so much that he had fallen into the paperback rack, spilling a heap of books across the floor. He jumped up to his feet as quickly as he could, and ran toward the glass entrance—the one that hadn't been boarded up. His heart pounded rapidly in his chest as he hid himself against the wall beside the doors.

Another series of gunshots erupted from the parking lot, and he tensed up at the sudden noise. He waited for a moment for the gunfire to subside, and then peered around the corner. Outside the entrance, there was a crowd of ghouls with their backs turned to the store. Luke moved out away from the wall to get a better view of what the creatures had focused their attention on. When he walked in front of the center door, he was able to see several vans and a few police cars. His heart jumped inside him as he spotted the team of troopers that were spread around the lot. All of the men had automatic weapons aimed at the building.

Suddenly, one of the squad members saw the young man through the glass, and he opened fired at the entrance. The glass in the entryway shattered as a rain of bullets crashed into the store. Other officers opened fire as well when they heard their team member's weapon go off.

Luke dropped to the floor as shards of broken glass rained down onto his body. A hail of bullets passed over his head, and he crawled along the tiles back toward the wall.

"Hold your fire!" Brent yelled to the other troopers, holding his hand up. "Hold your fire!" He walked over to Sergeant Harrison who was positioned behind the open door of a squad car.

"Yeah, Mathers?" the big black man said. "What you got?"

"I don't think the suspect is armed, sir," Brent said with a sense of urgency in his voice.

The sergeant glared at the shattered entrance for a moment, then looked back at the young officer. "Armed or not, we're authorized to shoot looters on sight."

Several zombies wandered into the store through the compromised entryway. The creatures stumbled right past Luke, completely unaware of his presence as they ambled off into the store.

"Hey, man!" Sean cried out as he ran through a check-out lane. "You all right?"

Luke brushed the shattered glass off his shirt and sat against the wall. He looked visibly shaken—his eyes darted about nervously and his breathing was heavy. His glasses hung crookedly on his nose, and one of the lenses was cracked.

"You all right, buddy?" Sean repeated, leaning against the wall next to the skinny, black-haired man.

"I'm okay," Luke replied. He stared blankly out into the store as he stroked his beard nervously.

"What's going on out there?" the red-haired man asked.

Luke's head jerked as he looked back over at the broken entryway. "A couple of cops," he gasped. "Nothing we can't handle."

"Cops?" Sean exclaimed.

Luke reached into his pants and pulled out the revolver that Scott had given him.

"What the hell are you doing?" Sean cried.

"This is our place now," the black-haired young man said, his eyes wild with fury. "They're not getting it—not without a fight."

"You're crazy!" Sean screamed. But it was too late. Luke had already jumped up and was walking across the entranceway. Sean reached out to grab him, but Luke lifted his arm quickly and fired several shots through the doorway.

A barrage of bullets suddenly ripped through the young, black-haired man's body as he fired again. The revolver clicked after he fired the sixth shot. He lowered the gun slowly, and looked down as more shots rang out from the parking lot. His chest was now full of bullet holes. He made a gurgling sound as he coughed up a mouthful of blood. The thick, red liquid ran down his chin and the revolver hung loosely from his twitching fingers. He staggered several steps back, gasping for air as sharp pains from his punctured lungs took hold of him.

"Jesus Christ!" Sean uttered in disbelief, and he backed into the wall.

Luke's body hit the floor face-down, and the gunfire came to a halt.

"You were saying, Mathers?" the big black man said to Brent. He rolled his eyes and lifted a bullhorn to his mouth.

"He wasn't armed before," Brent said to himself and shook his head. He leaned forward and aimed his pistol over the roof of a squad car at the building.

"We've got the building surrounded!" the sergeant barked into the bullhorn. "Come out now with your hands up!"

"Let's go, Samantha!" Mark yelled as he approached the young woman in the beauty department.

Samantha turned around, startled, and dropped a handheld mirror to the floor. Her face was made-up with dark eye shadow and lipstick, and her hair was pulled up into an elaborate hairstyle.

"Let's go," the big man repeated, grabbing hold of her arm. "Something's going on outside. We've gotta get to the stockroom."

The young woman quickly complied, and they dashed off into the aisles.

"Mathers," the sergeant said, taking cover behind a squad car. "We're going in. I need you to stay back and hold the parking lot."

Brent thought for a moment, stroking his mustache. "Let me go with you, sir."

The sergeant glanced at another officer, and the officer nodded, signaling that he would cover the parking lot.

"All right, Mathers," the big black man said, reaching into a nearby S.W.A.T. van. He retrieved an MP5 submachine gun and tossed it to the young officer. "Let's go."

Brent holstered his pistol and cocked the MP5. He got in line behind Sergeant Harrison, who led a team of officers toward the store entrance.

"Scott?" Joe gasped as he spotted the curled-up body on the stockroom floor. The container of Percocet lay on its side next to Scott. Pills were strewn about on the floor.

"You okay?" the blonde-haired man asked, and he knelt down beside the motionless body of his friend. He rolled the body over, and noticed that Scott's eyes were wide-open—which were covered with a milky-white film. He turned his head in aversion as he realized that his friend was dead.

Suddenly, a cold hand gripped tightly onto Joe's arm. He looked back down and saw Scott staring up at him with a vacant expression on his face.

"Jesus!" the blonde haired man gasped, and he jumped up, pulling his arm from the stiff grip of the corpse. He backed away from Scott's body without taking an eye off of it. As he took a step back, he tripped over a small stack of boxes and landed next to his rifle. He quickly snatched up the gun and aimed it at the corpse's head. But when he squeezed the trigger, it only made a clicking noise—the gun wasn't loaded. He scrambled over to the nearby box of ammo as the corpse began to rise slowly to its feet.

Suddenly, the double-doors burst open and Mark and Samantha rushed into the stockroom.

"What are you doing?" Mark exclaimed when he saw Joe loading a bullet into the rifle. Then he turned his head and caught site of his brother who was approaching the blonde-haired man.

Samantha screamed when she saw the pale skin and milky white eyes of Scott's animated corpse.

"No!" Mark cried as Joe took aim at his brother. He smashed his fist into the blonde-haired man's face, causing Joe to lose his balance. Then he rushed in front of his brother and stood between him and Joe with his arms out to block him from taking a shot.

Suddenly, the corpse grabbed the big man from behind, and bit him in the shoulder, ripping out a large chunk of flesh in its mouth. Mark screamed as blood spurted out from the wound.

Joe took aim again and fired a deafening blast at the corpse's head. The bullet smashed through its skull between the eyes, and blood splattered out all over Mark's back. Mark stumbled forward into Joe's arms as the corpse fell limply to the concrete floor behind him.

"Oh my God!" Samantha screamed, and she rushed to the big man's side. Tears streamed down her cheeks as she stared into Mark's eyes. She shook her head in disbelief, crying uncontrollably.

Joe held Mark in his arms for a moment, but the weight was too much for him. The big man fell from his grasp and collapsed onto the concrete floor.

Suddenly, Sean rushed into the room through the double-doors. He froze in his tracks when he saw the two bodies on the floor.

Joe knelt down at the big man's side and placed his hand on his forehead. Mark was still breathing, but he was gasping for air.

"We've got to get out of here!" Sean cried.

Joe tried to help the big man up, but he pushed his hand away.

"I'm not going," Mark gasped.

"No!" Samantha screamed. "You're coming with us!" She tugged on the big man's arm with all her might, but he wouldn't budge.

"Where's Luke?" Joe asked Sean.

The red-haired man gave him a somber look, but failed to respond.

Joe sighed deeply, and his eyed welled up with tears. "Well…let's go."

Samantha stayed at the big man's side, holding his hand as the other two men grabbed their guns. With tears in her eyes, she gave him a tender kiss on the cheek. Then she picked up her rifle and joined the other two survivors at the roll-down doors at the loading docks in the rear of the stockroom.

Sean pulled the rope up at the bottom of the rolling door. Bright sunlight filled the room as the door slid open with a loud sound. The gold van was parked on the ramp that led down from the loading door into the rear lot. A small crowd of zombies had convened on both sides of the ramp.

"Come on," Sean cried as he cranked the engine. "Jump in!"

Joe and Samantha hopped in the backseat, and the van rolled slowly down the ramp. When it leveled off on the concrete lot below, Sean stepped on the gas. The tires peeled out, and the van sped off through the parking lot, running down corpses in its wake.

"Where will we go?" Samantha asked, peering out though the back window at the crowd of zombies in the parking lot. The was a small group of police officers in front of the store, but they were busy fighting off the creatures to notice the van as it sped along the perimeter of the lot.

"Wherever the road takes us," Sean said, as the van drove off onto the main road, heading east.

Mark drew his handgun as he lay on the concrete floor. Blood poured out from his neck wound, forming a pool of red liquid on the floor beside him. He pulled the sliding mechanism on the Glock, cocking the hammer back. He could hear the distant voices of police officers the double-doors, and he held the gun up. He gazed over at his brother's body with tears in his eyes, waiting for the end.

Sergeant Harrison rushed through the main aisle of the store with a team of officers, including Brent Mathers, following closely behind. He signaled the men to stop as they reached the doorway to the stockroom. The men took up positions on each side of the doors, and the sergeant raised his weapon out in front. He gave the other officers a familiar gesture, signaling for them to cover him. Then he pushed the double-doors open with a powerful kick.

As soon as the doors opened, a loud gunshot erupted from the other side, and a single bullet smashed through the forehead of Sergeant Harrison. He fell to his knees for a moment, staring in shock at the large man on the floor of the stockroom with wide eyes. A confused expression crossed his face as his body wavered back and forth several times on its knees, then fell face-down onto the floor.

Brent and the other officers opened fire with their automatic pistols and submachine guns, and a rain of bullets filled the body of the large, curly-haired man. His body convulsed violently for a moment as blood splattered out in all directions, covering the surrounding boxes. Then he became still, and his eyes stared vacantly at the ceiling.

"Christ," Brent said as he walked into the stockroom. He looked back at the sergeant's body as the other men rushed into the room. As he scanned the area around him, he spotted a mob of zombies lurching toward them though the main aisle of the store.

"Looks like we're on our own," Brent said to the other officers. "Let's take what we need and get the hell outta here!"

A team of troopers hastily gathered up some supplies into large carts, and wheeled them toward the font entrance of the store. But as they wheeled the carts toward the vehicles in the parking lot, they were met with an unpleasant surprise. The lot was now filled with the terrible creatures, and the officers that had stayed back to cover the parking lot had perished. Hordes of ghouls were feasting on the flesh of the fallen officers, and several of the officers had already reanimated.

"Shit," Brent cursed as he reloaded his submachine gun. He and the other officers opened fire on the crowd of ghouls, dropping them on by one, until the mob of creatures had dispersed enough for the men to get into their vehicles.

As the last cart was loaded up, Brent watched from the window of Harrison's squad car as the creatures overran the store. To the young officer, it looked like a crazy shopping spree as the swarm of ghouls flooded into the store. For some strange reason, the mindless creatures wanted to be inside the glamorous, merchandise-filled store. It was almost as if they were driven by a distant memory from their former lives. A shiver ran up Brent's spine as he forced the thought from his mind.

"You guys go on ahead," Brent said to one of the other officers, as he stared off into the distance. "I'll catch up later." He peered through a pair of binoculars at the top of the hill in front of the store. A gold van, barely visible in the dimming light, disappeared over the hill, heading east.

"You sure?" one of the officers asked, a puzzled look crossing his face.

"Yeah. I should be back at the station later tonight. If not, don't come looking for me."

The other officers watched as Brent cranked the engine of Harrison's squad car and sped off through the parking lot, turning east when he reached the parkway. More zombies emerged from the streets and trees surrounding the large store, attracted by loud noises from the gunfire and the engines of the cars. Seeing the growing crowd of undead monsters, the remaining officers quickly cranked their engines and headed toward the main road.

A lone zombie with dark hair stared blankly at the squad cars from the entrance to the store. Its chest was full of bullet holes, and thick blood covered its shirt. A pair of plastic-rimmed glasses with cracked lenses hung crookedly on its nose. The creature let out a long, ghastly moan as a revolver dropped to the floor from its stiff fingers.

The convoy of vehicles drove off as the last rays of the evening sun peaked over the horizon, casting an orange glow upon the massive building. The former super-center of bustling commerce stood quietly in the late evening, peacefully mute to the horrors that had taken place between its walls that very day. It was truly an eve to remember—an eve of the dead.

Printed in the United Kingdom
by Lightning Source UK Ltd.
126315UK00003B/96/A